Emergency Contact

C.G. Macington

Table of Contents

Act 1

Chapter 1

Liam

The monitor beeps a steady rhythm—a counterpoint to the controlled chaos of Metropolitan General's emergency department. I check the ECG readout, nod, and make a note in the patient's chart.

"Your heart looks good, Mr. Reeves. We'll keep you for observation overnight, but I'm not seeing anything concerning in your tests."

The elderly man clutches his chest. "But the pain was real, Doc. Felt like an elephant sitting on me."

"I believe you." I pat his shoulder. "Sometimes anxiety can mimic heart attack symptoms. We'll run a few more tests to be certain."

I pull the curtain closed as I exit the bay, scanning the department. Three minor cases in the waiting room, two patients awaiting discharge, one waiting on psych consult. A manageable Tuesday morning.

Nurse Chen approaches with a tablet. "Labs back on bay four. Potassium's low."

"Start him on a replacement protocol. I'll check in after I review these scans." I swipe through digital images of a teenager's ankle. "Hairline fracture. Let's get ortho down here."

This is my element—the ordered disorder of emergency medicine. Patterns within chaos. Problems with solutions. No messy emotions or relationship complications, just clinical puzzles needing my expertise.

Three years as attending physician at Metro General, and I've perfected my routine. Work, sleep, occasional run, repeat. Simple. Safe.

"Dr. Winters to trauma bay one. Dr. Winters, trauma bay one." The overhead page interrupts my thoughts.

I hand the tablet back to Chen. "Tell radiology I'll call them back."

The trauma bay is already prepping when I arrive. Trauma nurses setting up IV lines, respiratory therapists checking ventilation equipment. I grab a trauma gown and gloves.

"What's coming?" I ask the charge nurse.

"Multi-vehicle collision on the highway. We're getting two critical patients. First ambulance three minutes out."

I nod, mentally shifting gears. "Let's get two units of O-neg on standby and alert CT they'll need to clear the scanner."

The trauma team assembles—a well-oiled machine I've helped build. No room for error. No space for distraction. Just the pure focus of keeping someone alive.

The ambulance bay doors burst open. Paramedics rush in wheeling a stretcher, one riding the gurney performing chest compressions.

"Thirty-year-old male, unrestrained driver. Found unconscious at the scene with multiple traumatic injuries. BP 80/40, tachy at 140. GCS 6 on arrival, dropped to 3 during transport. We've intubated, two large-bore IVs running wide open."

I step to the head of the bed. "On my count. One, two, three."

We transfer the patient to our trauma bed. Blood soaks through his clothes. His face is barely recognizable beneath lacerations and swelling.

"Start the massive transfusion protocol. I need a FAST scan now."

My hands move automatically—checking pupils, assessing breath sounds, palpating the abdomen. The ultrasound shows free fluid in the abdomen. Internal bleeding.

"He needs an OR now. Call surgery."

The doors burst open again. "Second victim coming in!"

"Chen, stay with this patient. I'll take the next." I strip off my bloody gloves, replacing them with fresh ones as the second gurney rolls in.

"Twenty-eight-year-old female, restrained passenger in the same vehicle. Multiple fractures, possible pneumothorax, pregnant approximately 30 weeks gestation. BP stable but fetal heart tones concerning at 100."

My stomach tightens. Two patients—mother and unborn child.

"Get OB down here stat." I lean over the woman. Her eyes flutter open, panicked. "Ma'am, you're in the hospital. We're taking care of you."

"James," she whispers. "My husband..."

"We're taking care of him too," I say, not revealing that her husband is coding in the next bay.

The ultrasound confirms a collapsed lung. "I need a chest tube tray." I turn to the resident beside me. "Have you done one before?"

"Twice," she answers.

"You're doing this one. I'll guide you."

While the resident prepares, I check the fetal monitor. Heart rate dropping. The OB attending rushes in.

"Fetal bradycardia," I report. "Mother has pneumothorax, multiple fractures, but vitals holding."

"We need to get her to the OR," the OB says. "Emergency C-section."

The resident looks up from prepping the chest tube. "But the pneumothorax—"

"Do it now," I direct. "She needs that chest tube before surgery."

The department doors swing open again. "We've got three more incoming!"

I glance at the trauma board. All bays full. "Move non-critical patients to the hallway. Call in the backup team."

For the next hour, I move between patients—intubating, placing central lines, calling consults. The department transforms into a battlefield hospital. I direct resources, make split-second decisions, work to save as many as we can.

The first patient, James, doesn't make it. Too much blood loss, too much trauma. I'll have to tell his pregnant wife when she wakes up from surgery. Her baby survived—barely—now in NICU fighting its own battle.

By hour three, I've lost track of how many patients I've touched. My scrubs are stained with other people's blood. My back aches from bending over beds. But we've stabilized the situation. Four patients in surgery, two transferred to ICU, one pronounced.

I step into the doctor's lounge, dropping onto a chair. My hands shake slightly as I reach for a cup of coffee. The adrenaline crash is coming.

This is why I became a doctor. Not for the routine ankle fractures or chest pain workups, but for days like today—when my decisions and actions make the immediate difference between life and death. Clean, clear purpose. No ambiguity.

I close my eyes for just a moment, allowing myself five seconds of exhaustion before heading back out. There are still patients waiting, charts to complete, families to update.

The door opens. "Dr. Winters?" It's Chen. "The trauma surgeon needs you in OR 2. The pregnant woman is crashing."

I set down my untouched coffee and stand. Back into the fray.

* * *

Noah

I wheel the gurney through the automatic doors of Metropolitan General's emergency department, my muscles burning from the sprint from the ambulance bay. The patient, a middle-aged man with a construction rod impaled through his thigh, groans despite the fentanyl we pushed en route.

"Male, 42, construction accident, impalement injury to right thigh with significant blood loss. BP 90/60, heart rate 130, oxygen 94% on 15 liters. Two large-bore IVs established, one liter of saline infusing, 100 micrograms fentanyl on board." I deliver the report while scanning the trauma bay, taking in the organized chaos.

That's when I see him.

Across the room, a doctor in navy scrubs looks up from another patient. His eyes—intense, focused—lock with mine for a fraction of a second. Something electric passes between us, a current I can't explain. The world narrows to just this moment, this connection, before reality crashes back in.

"Trauma bay three," a nurse directs, breaking the spell.

I nod and redirect the gurney, but I'm hyperaware of the doctor's presence as he finishes with his patient and moves toward us. His name badge reads "Dr. Winters."

"What do we have?" His voice is deep, controlled.

I repeat my report as we transfer the patient, adding details about the mechanism of injury. Dr. Winters nods, already assessing the impalement.

"Let's get two units O-neg, trauma panel, and portable X-ray. We need to see what vessels might be compromised before we touch that rod."

A young resident fumbles with the ultrasound machine, dropping the gel. Another struggles to place a third IV, missing twice on a visible vein.

Dr. Winters' jaw tightens. "We need access now."

Without thinking, I reach for the IV kit. "I can get it."

His eyes meet mine again—surprise, then something like recognition passing between us. He nods once.

I find a vein in the patient's forearm, sliding the catheter in smoothly on the first attempt. When I look up, Dr. Winters is already reaching for the fluids I've connected, hanging them without a word passing between us.

The patient's blood pressure drops suddenly. "70/40," calls out the monitor tech.

"He's bleeding around the rod," Dr. Winters says, his hands already moving to apply pressure.

I reach for the pressure bandages before he asks, positioning them exactly where needed. Our hands work in tandem, no instructions necessary.

"Need to transfuse faster," he mutters, and I'm already reaching for the rapid infuser, setting it up while he maintains pressure.

The resident stands frozen, watching us work. "Should I—"

"Call vascular and prep for OR," Dr. Winters directs without looking up. His focus is complete, but somehow I sense his next moves before he makes them.

I adjust the lighting without being asked. Hand him instruments before he reaches. Anticipate each step in the resuscitation as if we've worked together for years instead of minutes.

"Pressure's coming up. 90 systolic," I report, watching the monitors.

Dr. Winters nods. "Good work with those pressure bandages. Exactly where they needed to be."

Our eyes meet again over the patient. There's a question in his—the same one I feel. How is this possible? This synchronicity, this wordless understanding.

The vascular surgeon arrives, breaking the moment. As they prepare to move the patient to surgery, Dr. Winters steps back, his gaze finding mine again.

"You're new," he says. Not a question.

"Noah Bennet. Just transferred last week."

He studies me with an intensity that should feel uncomfortable but somehow doesn't. "You work well under pressure."

"So do you."

The corner of his mouth twitches—almost a smile. "I haven't seen many paramedics step in like that."

"I haven't seen many doctors who would let them."

This time, the smile emerges fully, transforming his face. Something flutters in my chest.

"They're ready for him upstairs," a nurse interrupts.

We help transfer the patient to the transport gurney. As they wheel him toward the elevator, Dr. Winters turns to me.

"Thanks for the assist." His voice is professional, but his eyes say something more.

"Anytime, Doctor." I hold his gaze a moment longer than necessary.

"Liam," he corrects, surprising himself with the informality.

"Liam," I repeat, testing the name. It feels right somehow, familiar on my tongue.

The trauma phone rings again, pulling him away. He hesitates, looking back at me with that same puzzled recognition I feel coursing through me.

"I'll be seeing you, Noah," he says tentatively shaking my hand before answering the call.

As I head back to my rig, I try to make sense of what just happened. I've worked with hundreds of doctors over my career, but never experienced anything like this—this immediate understanding, this unspoken communication.

It was like we'd done this dance before, in another life perhaps. Like my hands knew what his mind was thinking before he spoke it. Like we were two parts of the same medical machine, working in perfect harmony.

More than that, though, was the connection I felt when our eyes met. Recognition. Resonance. Something I can't explain but can't deny either.

I climb into the ambulance, my partner already starting the engine for our next call. But my mind stays in that trauma bay, with the doctor whose rhythm matched mine perfectly, whose eyes held questions I suddenly need answers to.

Liam Winters. Something tells me our paths are meant to cross again—and soon.

***

Liam

The doors swing shut behind Noah, and I'm left staring at the empty space where he stood. My hands hover mid-air, still warm from our brief contact. What just happened?

"Dr. Winters, we need you in Trauma 3!"

A nurse's voice snaps me back to reality. I blink, clearing my head of whatever strange spell Noah Bennet cast over me.

"On my way," I call back, already moving.

Trauma 3 holds a woman in her fifties, face ashen gray, lips tinged blue. The monitor shows ventricular tachycardia—a lethal heart rhythm if not addressed immediately.

"What's her story?" I ask, pulling on fresh gloves.

"Carol Mendez, 54, collapsed at home. Husband found her unresponsive. Paramedics got ROSC in the field but she's crashing again," the charge nurse reports.

I scan the monitors—blood pressure bottoming out, oxygen saturation plummeting. Her heart is failing.

"She's going into V-fib! Starting CPR," a resident announces, already compressing the woman's chest.

"Push one of epi," I order, moving to the head of the bed. "Let's get the ultrasound."

My hands move with practiced precision, but my mind splits in two—one half focused on the dying woman before me, the other drifting back to Noah's eyes, to that bizarre sense of recognition.

The resident pauses compressions as I position the ultrasound probe on the patient's chest. The heart barely contracts, a weak, fluttering motion.

"Tamponade," I announce, spotting the telltale collection of fluid around the heart. "Prep for pericardiocentesis."

As I reach for the pericardiocentesis tray, I feel a phantom presence beside me—as if Noah stands at my shoulder, anticipating my next move. The sensation is so vivid I almost turn to look.

"Dr. Winters?" The resident's voice sounds concerned.

I refocus. "Prepping for pericardial tap. Continue compressions."

The needle slides between my fingers, and for a split second, I hesitate. This never happens. My hands never hesitate.

What is wrong with me?

I take a steadying breath and guide the needle toward the patient's heart, feeling for the right spot with practiced fingers. The sensation when the needle penetrates the pericardial sac is unmistakable. Dark, bloody fluid fills the syringe.

"Got it," I murmur, more to myself than anyone else.

As the pressure around Carol's heart decreases, the monitors begin to show improvement. Her blood pressure inches up. The resident continues compressions while I drain the fluid.

"Hold compressions," I order after another minute. "Let's see what we've got."

The room falls silent as we watch the monitor. A beat. Then another. Irregular at first, then steadying.

"We have a rhythm," the nurse announces. "BP coming up."

Relief floods the room, but I remain tense, waiting for the other shoe to drop. It doesn't. Carol's vitals continue to stabilize.

"Nice save, Dr. Winters," the resident says, wiping sweat from her brow.

I nod, distracted. "Let's get cardiology down here and order an emergency echo. I want to know what caused the tamponade."

As the team moves to follow my instructions, I step back, stripping off my gloves. My hands are steady now, but something inside me trembles.

Noah's face flashes in my mind again—his easy confidence, the way he handed me instruments before I asked, how his eyes locked with mine in perfect understanding.

I escape to the staff bathroom, splashing cold water on my face. The man in the mirror looks haunted, water dripping from his stubbled chin.

"Get it together," I mutter to my reflection.

But the feeling persists—like a door long closed has cracked open, letting in a draft that disturbs the careful order of my life. Working with Noah felt like...coming home. Like finding a missing piece I hadn't realized was gone.

I dry my face with rough paper towels, the abrasion grounding me in reality. This is ridiculous. I met the man for all of twenty minutes. We worked well together—that happens sometimes in emergency medicine. The adrenaline, the high-stakes environment—it creates false intimacy.

That's all this is. It has to be.

Back at the nurses' station, I update Carol's chart, forcing myself to focus on each keystroke. The familiar routine of documentation should calm me, but my mind keeps drifting.

What if I run into Noah again? The thought sends an electric current through my chest. What if I don't? That possibility feels even worse.

"Earth to Dr. Winters." My colleague Dr. Chen waves a hand in front of my face. "You planning to finish that chart today?"

I blink, realizing I've been staring at the same screen for minutes. "Sorry. Long day."

She leans against the counter. "You okay? You seem...off."

"Fine. Just tired." The lie comes easily.

Chen doesn't look convinced but lets it drop. "The Mendez case was impressive. Not many people would have caught that tamponade so quickly."

"Just did what needed doing." I close the chart and stand up. "I'm going to check on her."

As I walk to Carol's room, now stabilized and waiting for transfer to the cardiac ICU, I realize I'm scanning the ED for a familiar face. For Noah. The realization stops me cold.

I've spent years building walls around myself after Jason left. Years cultivating professional detachment, keeping colleagues at arm's length. And now one paramedic with knowing eyes has me questioning everything.

I check Carol's vitals, confirm her transfer is on track, and retreat to the doctors' lounge. The coffee is burnt and bitter, but I drink it anyway, needing something to do with my hands.

For years, I've functioned perfectly well by keeping my emotions locked down tight. Emotions cloud judgment, and in emergency medicine, clear judgment saves lives. I've built my entire identity around being the doctor who stays calm, who never gets rattled.

But Noah rattled me. In twenty minutes, he cracked foundations I thought were solid concrete.

I don't know if I can handle that. Don't know if I want to.

The lounge door opens, and I tense, irrationally hoping and fearing it might be him.

Chapter 2

Liam

It's Dr. Kapoor who walks in, not Noah. She heads straight for the coffee machine, grimacing at the dark sludge inside.

"That looks lethal," she comments, pouring herself a cup anyway.

"Hey Mira, probably is." I check my watch. My shift ended twenty minutes ago, but I can't bring myself to leave yet. "How's the Mendez transfer going?"

"Smooth. Cardiology's taking good care of her." She sits across from me, studying my face. "You know, you could go home. We've got things covered."

I nod absently, turning my empty cup in my hands. "Just finishing up some paperwork."

It's a lie. My paperwork is done. I'm lingering because... because what? On the off chance Noah might return with another patient? Pathetic.

"Right." Kapoor's tone says she doesn't believe me. "Well, don't forget about the EMS meeting tomorrow. Nine AM sharp."

I frown. "EMS meeting?"

"The quarterly review? With all the paramedic supervisors?" She raises an eyebrow. "Please tell me you didn't forget. You're the medical director."

The EMS medical director position. Right. I'd taken it on six months ago when Dr. Levinson retired. It mostly involves reviewing protocols, signing off on continuing education, and quarterly meetings with the paramedic supervisors to discuss any issues between the hospital and emergency services.

"Of course not," I lie again. "Nine AM. Conference room B."

"Conference room A," she corrects. "They moved it, remember? Sent an email last week."

"Right. A." I stand up, tossing my cup in the trash. "I should head out."

As I change in the locker room, I mentally review my responsibilities for tomorrow's meeting. Nothing complex—just routine updates and addressing any concerns from the field. I've prepared the slides already. It'll be fine.

* * *

It's not fine.

I arrive at Conference Room A fifteen minutes early, coffee in hand, laptop open to review my presentation one last time. The room is empty, which is exactly how I like it. Time to center myself, organize my thoughts.

The door opens at 8:50. I look up, expecting to see one of the paramedic supervisors I've worked with before.

Instead, Noah Bennet walks in.

He's wearing a crisp blue uniform shirt with paramedic patches and supervisor stripes. His dark hair is slightly damp, like he's just showered, and he carries a leather portfolio under one arm. He stops short when he sees me, surprise flickering across his face before it transforms into a warm smile.

"Dr. Winters." He crosses the room, hand extended. "Good to see you again."

I stand on autopilot, taking his hand. The same electric current from yesterday zips through me at the contact. "Bennet. You're... a supervisor?"

"Just promoted last month." His hand lingers in mine a beat too long before releasing. "I transferred from County General's system. This is my first meeting here."

Of course. Of course he's under my supervision now. Because the universe apparently has a twisted sense of humor.

"Congratulations on the promotion." My voice sounds distant to my own ears.

"Thanks." He sets his portfolio on the table, taking the seat directly to my right. Close enough that I catch the clean scent of his soap. "I've been looking forward to working with you in this capacity. Your reputation precedes you."

"Does it?" I take a sip of coffee to hide whatever expression might be trying to form on my face.

"Absolutely. The paramedics all say you're the best medical director they've had. Fair, knowledgeable, willing to listen to concerns from the field."

Before I can respond, the door opens again as other supervisors begin filing in. I recognize most of them—Martinez from the west side station, Thompson from downtown, Chen from the south district. They greet me with familiar nods, then turn curious eyes to Noah.

I clear my throat. "Everyone, this is Supervisor Bennet. He's transferred in from County to take over the east district."

Noah stands, shaking hands all around, instantly at ease in a way I've never managed. He laughs at something Martinez says, and the sound does something strange to my chest.

I busy myself with my laptop, pulling up the presentation slides while trying to ignore Noah's presence beside me. It's impossible. Every movement, every breath he takes registers on my awareness like a blip on radar.

The meeting begins. I go through the slides mechanically, discussing protocol updates, reviewing response times, addressing equipment concerns. On the surface, I'm the consummate professional—calm, articulate, focused.

Inside, I'm a mess.

Noah asks insightful questions. He offers thoughtful suggestions about improving handoffs between paramedics and ED staff. At one point, he builds on an idea I present before I've fully articulated it—just like yesterday, anticipating my thoughts before I voice them.

The other supervisors notice. I catch Thompson and Martinez exchanging glances when Noah completes my sentence about a new medication protocol.

"Exactly," I say, trying to sound normal. "That's precisely what I was thinking."

Noah smiles, a quick flash of understanding passing between us. "Great minds."

The meeting wraps up after an hour. As the supervisors gather their things, Noah lingers, organizing his notes with deliberate slowness.

When we're the only two left, he turns to me. "So, I guess we'll be working together regularly now."

"Looks that way." I focus on shutting down my laptop, avoiding his eyes.

"I'm glad." His voice drops lower, more personal. "Yesterday was... something else."

I finally look up, meeting his gaze. The connection from yesterday snaps back into place immediately, like a circuit completing. "Yes. It was."

"I've never experienced anything like that before." He leans slightly closer. "The way we worked together. It was like—"

"We'd done it a thousand times before," I finish.

He nods, eyes never leaving mine. "Exactly."

"I should get back to the ED," I say, gathering my laptop. The sensible choice. The safe one.

"Actually..." Noah rubs the back of his neck. "I was wondering if you wanted to grab some coffee from the cafeteria first? If you have time, that is."

My immediate instinct is to decline. I have charts to review, patients to check on, a department to run. Perfect excuses.

But something in his expression—hopeful, open—makes the refusal die in my throat.

"Sure." The word escapes before I can catch it. "I have about twenty minutes before my next meeting."

Noah's face lights up with a smile so genuine it almost hurts to look at. "Great! That's—that's great."

His enthusiasm catches me off guard. It's just coffee in a hospital cafeteria, not exactly a five-star experience. Yet he's practically beaming as we walk together down the corridor.

"I've been meaning to try the coffee here anyway," he says as we wait for the elevator. "At County, it was basically brown water. Had to bring my own from home to survive."

"Don't get your hopes up. Ours isn't winning any awards either."

The elevator arrives, and we step in. It's empty except for us, and suddenly the space feels much smaller than it should. Noah stands close enough that I can smell his aftershave—something clean and subtle with notes of cedar.

"I'll be the judge of that," he says. "I've developed quite the palate after years of terrible hospital coffee."

The cafeteria is half-full, mostly with staff grabbing late breakfasts or early lunches. We get our coffees—I take mine black, Noah adds cream and sugar to his—and find a small table in the corner.

"So," Noah says after taking a sip and making an exaggerated face of consideration, "verdict's in. Slightly better than County, but that's a low bar."

I find myself smiling despite my nervousness. "Told you."

"Worth it for the company, though."

The comment hangs between us, unexpectedly intimate. I focus on my coffee cup, turning it slowly between my palms.

"How long have you been at Metropolitan?" Noah asks, mercifully changing the subject.

"Three years as an attending. I moved here from Ottawa before that."

"You must know this place inside and out."

"Pretty much. It's home now." I pause, realizing how true that is. "What about you? Before County?"

"Started out in Calgary right after paramedic school. Worked there for five years, then Vancouver for three, then County for two." He shrugs. "I've moved around a bit."

"Any particular reason?"

Something flickers across his face—a shadow of something deeper. "My brother Matt died when I was twenty-two. Car accident. After that, I had trouble staying in one place too long."

The personal revelation catches me off guard. "I'm sorry about your brother."

"Thanks. It's what got me into emergency medicine, actually. The paramedics who responded to his accident... they did everything right. He just had injuries that weren't survivable. But I saw how they tried, how they treated him with dignity even when it was clear he wouldn't make it." Noah's eyes meet mine. "I wanted to be that for someone else."

The honesty in his voice touches something in me. "That's... that's a powerful motivation."

"What about you? Why emergency medicine?"

I consider giving my standard answer—the one about loving the challenge and variety. Instead, I find myself saying, "I like fixing things that are broken. In the moment. Immediate results."

"And people?"

"What about them?"

"Do you like fixing broken people too?"

The question hits closer to home than I'm comfortable with. "People are more complicated than medical problems."

Noah studies me over the rim of his coffee cup. "True. But sometimes more rewarding when you get it right."

There's a weight to his words that makes my chest tighten. The air between us feels charged, like the atmosphere before a storm.

"What made you transfer to Metropolitan?" I ask, desperate to redirect.

"Needed a change. County was getting..." He pauses, searching for the right word. "Stagnant. And I'd heard good things about the program here."

"From?"

"Around." He smiles, something playful in his expression. "Plus, turns out the medical director is pretty impressive."

Heat rises to my face. Before I can respond, my phone buzzes. I check it, almost relieved for the interruption.

"Emergency?" Noah asks.

I nod, already standing. "Trauma coming in. Multiple GSWs."

"Duty calls." He stands too. "Rain check on finishing our coffee?"

"Yeah." I hesitate, torn between the pull I feel toward him and the safety of professional distance. "I should go."

"Liam." My first name in his voice stops me. "Yesterday wasn't a fluke. What happened between us in that trauma room—that connection—it doesn't just happen."

I meet his eyes, unable to deny the truth of what he's saying. "I know."

"Good." He smiles again, softer this time. "Go save lives, Dr. Winters. I'll see you around."

I turn and hurry toward the ED, my mind already shifting to the incoming trauma, but part of me remains in that cafeteria, sitting across from Noah Bennet and the possibilities he represents.

Chapter 3

Noah

"Thirty-year-old male, GSW to the abdomen, BP 90/60, heart rate 120, decreased breath sounds on the left." I relay the information to the trauma team as we wheel the gurney through Metropolitan General's emergency department doors. My partner Dani and I transfer our patient to the waiting trauma bay where Dr. Chen—not Liam—stands ready with her team.

A pang of disappointment hits me harder than expected. I scan the room instinctively, searching for those intense eyes and steady hands that worked alongside mine so perfectly last time.

"Where do you need us, Dr. Chen?" I ask, maintaining professional focus despite the hollow feeling in my chest.

"We're good here, thanks. You can clear for your next call," she says, already focused on the patient.

I help transfer monitors and give my final report, but something feels off. The handoff lacks the seamless rhythm I experienced with Liam. Working with Dr. Chen is fine—she's competent and direct—but there's no silent communication, no anticipating each other's next move.

"Coming, Bennet?" Dani calls from the doorway, radio already squawking with another dispatch.

"Yeah, just finishing up." I strip off my gloves and follow her out, throwing one last glance over my shoulder at the trauma bay.

Back in the rig, Dani raises an eyebrow at me. "You okay? You seem distracted."

"I'm fine." I wipe down equipment with more force than necessary. "Just thinking about the protocols we discussed at yesterday's meeting."

"Uh-huh." She doesn't sound convinced. "Nothing to do with a certain ER doctor who wasn't there today?"

My head snaps up. "What?"

"Come on, Noah. I saw how you two worked together on that construction accident last week. Like some weird medical mind-meld. Then you disappeared with him after yesterday's meeting."

"We just had coffee." I focus on restocking our supplies, avoiding her gaze.

"Sure." She grins, buckling her seatbelt as we pull away from the hospital. "And I'm just saying you looked like someone stole your puppy when Chen walked in instead of him."

I don't answer, but her observation rattles me. Have I really become so transparent? I've known Liam for all of two encounters, yet his absence left me feeling off-balance, like walking into a room and finding the furniture rearranged.

We spend the next few hours handling routine calls—a fall at a nursing home, a diabetic with low blood sugar, a psychiatric transfer. My body goes through the motions while my mind keeps circling back to the same question: What is happening to me?

After dropping our last patient at County, we get cleared to return to base for shift change. I stare out the window as Dani drives, buildings blurring past.

"When Jake died," I say suddenly, surprising myself, "I promised I'd never miss something important again. That I'd always be present, always paying attention."

Dani glances over, giving me space to continue.

"But today, I wasn't fully there. I was looking for someone who wasn't even working. That's never happened to me before."

"You're human, Noah. Even with your freaky sixth sense for patient care."

I shake my head. "It's not just that. When I'm around Liam, everything clicks into place. Like we've done this dance a thousand times before. I've never experienced anything like it."

"So what's the problem? Sounds like something worth exploring."

"The problem is I've known him for about five minutes total, and I'm already disappointed when he's not around. That's not normal."

"Normal is overrated." Dani pulls into the station parking lot. "My grandma always said when something feels that right, that fast, you don't question it. You run toward it."

"Your grandma never met Dr. Liam Winters," I mutter.

"No, but she met my grandpa and married him three weeks later. They had fifty-two years together before he died." She parks and turns to face me. "Look, I'm not saying propose to the guy. Just... don't overthink it. Whatever this connection is, it's rare."

I nod, gathering my things as we exit the rig. "Thanks, Dani."

"Anytime, boss." She punches my arm lightly. "For what it's worth, he looked at you the same way."

Her words follow me into the station, where I mechanically complete my end-of-shift duties. I can't stop thinking about that moment in the cafeteria when Liam told me about choosing emergency medicine—the vulnerability in his eyes, quickly masked but unmistakably there.

In the locker room, I change out of my uniform, still puzzling over this unexpected pull toward him. I've dated before, felt attraction and even love, but never this immediate sense of recognition. Like finding a missing piece I didn't know was lost.

My phone buzzes with a text from an unknown number.

Sorry I missed you today. Had to cover at our satellite campus. You working tomorrow? - Liam

I stare at the screen, a smile spreading across my face. He noticed my absence too. Maybe I'm not the only one feeling this strange connection.

I type back: *Definitely. I'm sure we'll see each other soon.*

Whatever this is between us, I'm not running from it. For the first time since Jake died, I'm ready to follow my instincts toward something—someone—that feels inexplicably right.

* * *

Liam

I catch sight of Noah the moment he pushes through the ER doors. He's guiding a stretcher with an elderly woman who appears stable—elevated leg, conscious, talking. My heart performs that strange flutter I've been trying to diagnose in myself since our first meeting.

"Seventy-eight-year-old female, fall at home," Noah announces to the charge nurse. "Possible ankle fracture, vitals stable."

I busy myself with a chart, pretending I haven't noticed him. It's ridiculous—I'm a grown man, a physician with years of training, yet I'm acting like a nervous intern.

"Dr. Winters." Noah's voice carries across the department.

I look up, trying to appear casually professional. "Bennet. What have you got?"

He briefs me on the patient while we walk to bay three. I'm hyperaware of how our shoulders nearly touch, how his steps match mine without effort.

"Mrs. Lowell, I'm Dr. Winters," I introduce myself, examining the swollen ankle. "We'll get you some pain relief and X-rays right away."

"Such nice young men," Mrs. Lowell says, patting Noah's hand. "This one kept me laughing the whole ride over."

Noah smiles, and something tightens in my chest. "Just doing my job, ma'am."

I write orders for the ankle and turn to Noah. "Thanks for bringing her in. Doesn't look too complicated."

"Yeah, quiet shift so far." He lingers, clearly wanting to say more.

The awkward silence stretches between us until a monitor alarm shrieks from across the department.

"Code Blue, bay eight!" a nurse shouts.

I sprint toward the sound, aware of Noah following close behind. In bay eight, a middle-aged man convulses on the gurney, his monitor showing ventricular fibrillation.

"What happened?" I demand, pulling on gloves.

"Post-op cholecystectomy, discharged yesterday," the nurse explains, attaching defibrillator pads. "Came in with abdominal pain. Vitals were stable five minutes ago."

I scan the department for other physicians. No one. Dr. Chen is in trauma one, Dr. Kapoor left for a meeting, and the residents are in didactics.

"Shock at 200," I order, beginning compressions while the nurse charges the defibrillator.

"Clear!" Everyone steps back as the patient's body jerks with the current.

No conversion. I resume compressions, mind racing through possibilities. "Get me an ultrasound, now."

Noah positions the portable ultrasound before I even ask. I glance at him, startled by his anticipation, then focus on the screen.

"Cardiac tamponade," I mutter, seeing the telltale fluid around the heart. "He's bleeding into his pericardium. We need to drain it immediately."

The nurse hands me a pericardiocentesis kit. Time slows as I realize what we're facing—a complex, risky procedure with no backup.

"I need another set of hands," I say. "Someone who can—"

"I'm here." Noah steps forward, snapping on gloves. "Tell me what you need."

I hesitate. He's a paramedic, not a surgeon. But something in his steady gaze convinces me.

"I'll guide the needle into the pericardial sac. You'll need to hold the ultrasound perfectly still so I can visualize the approach."

Noah positions himself with the ultrasound probe, his hands rock-steady. "Ready when you are."

I insert the needle, watching its trajectory on the screen. "Two centimeters left... now straight in, slowly."

Noah adjusts the probe with uncanny precision, giving me the exact view I need. The needle advances into the pericardial space.

"Got it." Dark blood flows into the syringe. The patient's pressure immediately improves.

"We need to place a drain," I say. "This is temporary."

What happens next feels like a choreographed dance. Noah hands me each instrument before I ask, positions himself exactly where needed, and anticipates every move. When I need to secure the catheter, he's already prepared the suture.

"How did you know to load the needle driver that way?" I ask, bewildered.

"Just felt right." His eyes meet mine over our surgical masks.

The monitor shows a stable rhythm. The patient's color improves.

"We need to get him to surgery," I say, stepping back. "That was..."

"Yeah," Noah agrees. "It was."

The trauma team arrives to transport the patient. We stand in the aftermath, both breathing hard, both aware that what just happened wasn't normal.

In the staff bathroom, I wash blood from my hands. Noah enters, his scrub top splattered with evidence of our emergency procedure.

"You want to tell me how you knew exactly what to do in there?" I ask, watching him in the mirror.

He shrugs, turning on the faucet beside me. "I've assisted with chest tubes before, but nothing like that. I just... knew what you needed."

"That's not possible. The way you loaded that needle driver—that's a specific technique I learned from my mentor in residency. No one else does it that way."

Our eyes meet in the mirror. Water runs over our hands, forgotten.

"I can't explain it," Noah says quietly. "But I felt like I'd done it a hundred times before. With you."

The air between us charges with something electric. I turn off the water, reach for paper towels.

"This isn't normal," I say, voice low. "What's happening here."

"No," he agrees. "It's not."

Our fingers brush as he takes a towel from me. That same jolt, that same recognition.

"We saved him," Noah says. "Whatever this is—" he gestures between us, "—it works."

"It works," I echo, unable to deny the evidence. "But it doesn't make sense."

Noah steps closer. "Does it have to?"

My pager interrupts the moment, demanding my attention. I check it, grateful for the distraction.

"I have to go," I say, backing toward the door. "Patient in trauma one."

Noah nods, understanding. "Go. But Liam— "We should talk about this. Really talk."

"I know," I admit, pausing at the threshold. "We will."

As I walk away, I feel the pull of him like gravity, drawing me back. Whatever this connection is—this impossible synchronicity—it's becoming harder to ignore with each encounter.

* * *

Liam

I find Mira in the doctors' lounge, scrolling through patient charts on her tablet. The room is mercifully empty except for her, which is exactly what I need right now.

"Got a minute?" I ask, closing the door behind me.

She looks up, reading something in my expression that makes her set the tablet aside. "For you? Always. What's up?"

I sink into the chair across from her, unsure how to begin. How do you explain something you don't understand yourself?

"I'm experiencing something... unusual," I start, running a hand through my hair. "With one of the paramedic supervisors."

Mira's eyebrows shoot up. "Unusual how? Are we talking professionally unusual or personally unusual?"

"Both? Neither?" I exhale heavily. "It's Noah Bennet. The new supervisor."

"Tall guy? Great smile? I've seen him around." She leans forward. "What about him?"

"When we work together, it's like..." I struggle to find words that won't sound completely insane. "It's like we've worked together for years. He anticipates what I need before I ask. Knows techniques I've never shown him."

Mira tilts her head, confusion crossing her features.

"Today in trauma, he loaded a needle driver using a technique my mentor taught me in residency. A specific way that nobody else does. Nobody."

"Maybe he's worked with someone who—"

"No." I cut her off. "It's more than that. During a pericardiocentesis, he positioned the ultrasound perfectly without instruction. He handed me instruments before I asked. He knew exactly what I was going to do next."

Mira's expression shifts from confusion to concern. "Liam, are you getting enough sleep?"

"I know how it sounds." I lean forward, voice low. "But there's something happening between us. Some connection I can't explain."

"Connection?" She studies my face. "Like attraction?"

"That too," I admit, feeling heat rise to my face. "But this is different. It's like... déjà vu, but constant. Like we've known each other before."

Mira sits back, arms crossed. "You think you're what? Psychically linked with this paramedic you just met?"

When she puts it that way, it sounds ridiculous. I scrub my hands over my face. "I know it sounds crazy."

"It does," she agrees, then pauses. "But..."

I look up. "But what?"

"The nurses have been talking." She lowers her voice. "About you two. How you work together like you're reading each other's minds. Marina said watching you two in trauma was like watching a dance that had been rehearsed for years."

My heart rate picks up. "So it's not just me noticing this."

"Apparently not." Mira uncrosses her arms, leaning forward. "And you feel it too? This... connection?"

"Every time we're in the same room." I stare at my hands. "It's intense. Distracting. I can't focus when he's around, but when we're working together, it's like we're one person. It doesn't make sense."

"The human brain is a mystery," she says thoughtfully. "Maybe you're picking up on subtle cues from each other. Or maybe..." She trails off.

"Maybe what?"

She shrugs. "Maybe some connections defy explanation. My grandmother back in India would say your souls recognize each other."

I snort. "I don't believe in souls."

"Don't you?" She raises an eyebrow. "You believe in evidence. And from what you're telling me, the evidence suggests something extraordinary is happening."

She's right, and it unsettles me. I've built my life on logic, on things I can prove and explain. This... this is something else entirely.

"So what are you going to do about it?" Mira asks.

"I don't know." I sink back in my chair. "Ignore it? Hope it goes away?"

"Is that what you want? For it to go away?"

The question catches me off guard. Do I want this connection to disappear? The thought creates an unexpected hollow feeling in my chest.

"No," I admit quietly. "But I don't know what to do with it either. It's not just the professional aspect—which is weird enough. There's also..." I hesitate.

"The attraction," Mira finishes for me. "You're drawn to him."

"Yes." The admission feels like relief. "And that terrifies me. After Jason—"

"Jason was a selfish ass who put his career before everything else," Mira interrupts. "Not everyone is Jason."

"I know that. Logically, I know that." I sigh. "But this thing with Noah—it's not just attraction. It's like he can see inside me. And that's..."

"Terrifying," she supplies.

"Exactly."

Mira reaches across the table, squeezing my hand. "So what are you going to do?"

"I don't know," I repeat, the truth of it settling heavily between us. "Talk to him, I guess? Try to figure out what this is?"

"That would be the adult approach," she agrees with a small smile.

"Or I could just avoid him for the rest of my career," I suggest half-heartedly.

"Because that's worked so well for you so far?" Mira rolls her eyes. "The entire nursing staff is already gossiping about your supernatural connection. Avoidance isn't an option anymore."

She's right, and we both know it. Whatever is happening between Noah and me, it's not something I can outrun.

"Talk to him," Mira says gently. "Maybe there's a perfectly logical explanation."

"And if there isn't?"

She shrugs. "Then maybe you accept that not everything in life can be explained. And maybe that's okay."

Chapter 4

Liam

I've never been good at relaxing. Even on my days off, my mind tends to cycle through patient cases, administrative concerns, and the endless to-do list waiting for me when I return to the hospital. But after the week I've had, I need to try.

My apartment feels too quiet, too empty for proper decompression. The walls seem to echo with my thoughts, particularly ones about Noah Bennet and whatever inexplicable thing is happening between us. So I grab my laptop, planning to catch up on medical journals at the neighborhood coffee shop instead. At least there, the ambient noise might drown out the questions circling in my head.

The morning air is crisp as I walk the three blocks to Brewed Awakening. It's busy but not packed—perfect. I order my usual (black coffee, no room) and find a corner table partially hidden by a large potted fern. The isolation feels comforting.

I open my laptop and pull up the latest issue of the New England Journal of Medicine. The lead article discusses innovations in trauma care protocols—normally something that would capture my full attention. But today, the words blur together as my mind drifts.

What Mira said yesterday keeps replaying in my head. The nurses talking about Noah and me. Our "supernatural connection." The idea that our souls somehow recognize each other.

"Ridiculous," I mutter, taking a sip of coffee that's still too hot. The burn on my tongue is a welcome distraction.

I force myself to focus on the article, making notes on potential protocol adjustments for our department. After an hour, I've made decent progress, and the rational part of my brain has begun to reassert itself. Whatever I experienced with Noah must have a logical explanation. Perhaps we both trained under similar mentors. Maybe we've read the same research. Or possibly, I've been so sleep-deprived that my mind fabricated connections that weren't really there.

Yes, that's it. Sleep deprivation combined with an attraction I wasn't prepared for. Nothing supernatural about it.

I close the journal article and open my email, feeling more centered than I have in days. The strange connection with Noah Bennet was just my imagination. Next time I see him, things will be normal. Professional. As they should be.

"Dr. Winters?"

The voice hits me before I look up, and I know—I know—who it belongs to. My body reacts instantly: heart rate accelerating, skin warming, that same inexplicable sense of recognition washing over me.

Noah Bennet stands at my table, coffee in hand, looking as surprised as I feel. He's dressed in jeans and a simple gray henley that clings to his shoulders in a way his uniform never does. His dark hair is slightly tousled, as if he's been running his hands through it.

"Noah," I manage, my carefully reconstructed rationality crumbling. "What are you doing here?"

He gestures vaguely toward the counter. "Coffee? It's kind of what they sell here."

His smile reaches his eyes, creating tiny creases at the corners. I notice these details with alarming clarity.

"Mind if I join you?" he asks when I don't respond.

I should say no. I should make an excuse, pack up my things, and leave. Instead, I find myself closing my laptop and nodding toward the empty chair across from me.

"Please."

As Noah sits down, that familiar current passes between us. It's less intense than when we're working together in trauma, but unmistakably there—a subtle awareness of each other that defies explanation.

"I didn't expect to see you here," he says, taking a sip of his coffee—something with cinnamon, I can smell it from here. "Do you live nearby?"

"About three blocks west," I answer, then immediately wonder if I should have shared that. "You?"

"Just moved to an apartment on Maple, about five minutes from here." He glances at my closed laptop. "Working on your day off?"

"Just catching up on some reading." I wrap my hands around my mug, needing something to anchor me. "What about you? No shift today?"

"Off until tomorrow morning." Noah studies me for a moment, his expression thoughtful. "You look like you're feeling better than the last time I saw you. After the cardiac tamponade case."

The memory flashes between us—the intensity of working together, the way he anticipated my every move, our conversation in the staff bathroom afterward.

"I've been thinking about that," I say carefully.

"Me too." His voice drops slightly. "Non-stop, actually."

The honesty in his statement catches me off guard. I've been trying to rationalize what's happening between us, while he's been openly confronting it.

"I tried convincing myself it was all in my head," I admit. "That I was imagining this... connection."

Noah's eyes hold mine. "And now?"

I gesture between us. "Now you're here, in the coffee shop three blocks from my apartment, and I can feel it happening again."

"The connection."

"Yes."

Noah takes a slow breath. "So I'm not crazy."

"If you are, then we both are." I attempt a smile that feels more genuine than expected. "Along with the entire nursing staff, apparently."

"They've noticed too?" His eyebrows raise.

"According to my colleague Mira, we're the talk of the hospital." I shake my head, still finding it hard to believe. "She said watching us work together is like watching a choreographed dance."

Noah leans forward slightly. "That's exactly what it feels like from my end too. Like we've done this a thousand times before."

The validation of my experience sends a wave of both relief and apprehension through me. I'm not imagining things—but that means I have to face whatever this is.

Noah's eyes stay fixed on mine, his expression a mix of wonder and uncertainty. "So what do we do about it?" he asks, voice low enough that only I can hear. "This... whatever it is between us?"

The question hangs in the air. What should we do? I'm a doctor—I deal in diagnoses and treatments, in solutions and protocols. But for this? I have nothing.

"I don't know," I admit, running a hand through my hair. "Maybe we just... let it happen? See where it goes?" The suggestion sounds inadequate even to my own ears. "For all we know, it might just play itself out."

Noah nods slowly, considering. "Like an experiment?"

"A very unscientific one," I add with a small smile. "No control group, terrible methodology."

"And only two subjects." His smile mirrors mine, but his eyes remain serious. "I'm okay with that approach if you are."

I take a deep breath. "I am."

The tension between us shifts, not disappearing but transforming into something more comfortable. Noah takes a sip of his coffee, then sets it down with purpose.

"So, Dr. Winters, if we're going to let this play out, maybe we should actually get to know each other." He leans back in his chair. "Outside of trauma rooms and medical protocols."

"Fair enough." I wrap my fingers around my mug, drawing comfort from its warmth. "What do you want to know?"

"Everything," he says simply. "But let's start with why emergency medicine? What drew you to it apart from being able to fix things?"

It's a standard question, one I've answered countless times in interviews and at conferences. I have a polished response about the challenge and variety, about making immediate differences in critical moments. But looking at Noah, I find myself wanting to give him the real answer.

"My grandfather died of a heart attack when I was twelve," I say. "We were at his lake house. No neighbors for miles. By the time the ambulance arrived, it was too late." I pause, surprised by how fresh the memory still feels. "I remember standing there, watching these paramedics work on him, knowing exactly what they were doing but not why it wasn't working. I wanted to understand."

Noah nods, his expression reflecting a deep understanding that goes beyond sympathy. "That explains a lot about how you work. The intensity, the focus. I'm sorry about your grandfather."

"I'm sorry about your brother."

We sit in shared understanding for a moment. Then Noah asks, "You're not from here originally, right? Your accent has a slight Quebecois inflection sometimes."

I raise my eyebrows. "You picked up on that? Most people don't notice."

"I notice everything about you," he says, then looks slightly embarrassed by his own admission. "Sorry, that sounded—"

"No, it's okay." I find myself smiling. "You're right. I'm from Ottawa originally, the Gatineau side."

"What brought you here?"

The question is innocent enough, but it touches on everything I've been avoiding talking about. I should deflect, give the simplified version I tell everyone else—better opportunity, change of scenery. Instead, I hear myself saying:

"I needed to get away from Ottawa. From the hospital there. From Jason."

Noah doesn't push, just waits for me to continue, his presence somehow making it easier to keep talking.

"Jason was another doctor at the hospital where I worked. Cardiothoracic surgeon. Brilliant, charismatic." I pause, the memories flooding back. "We were together for three years. I thought we were building something real."

I take a sip of my now-lukewarm coffee, buying time.

"Turns out, he was building something with one of his residents too. And possibly a nurse from ICU." The bitterness in my voice surprises me. I thought I was past this. "When I confronted him, he acted like I was overreacting. Like exclusivity was something we'd never discussed, when we absolutely had."

Noah's expression darkens. "What an asshole."

The simple validation in those three words loosens something in my chest.

"The worst part wasn't even the cheating. It was realizing how much of myself I'd given up for him." The words tumble out now, things I haven't told anyone, not even Mira. "I changed my specialty focus because it aligned better with his schedule. Turned down a research opportunity because he thought it would take too much time away from us. Started dressing differently because he made comments about my 'academic look.'"

I shake my head, embarrassed by my own naivety. "After we broke up, I looked around and didn't recognize my life anymore. So I left. New hospital, new city, new start."

"And threw yourself into work instead," Noah says, not a question but an observation.

"Completely. It was safer that way." I let out a humorless laugh. "No relationship, no friends outside the hospital, just work. I convinced myself it was enough."

"And was it?"

I meet his gaze, struck by how easy it is to be honest with him. "No. But it was... manageable."

Noah nods, understanding in his eyes. "Until now?"

The question hangs between us, loaded with implications neither of us is ready to fully address.

"Until now," I agree quietly.

* * *

Noah

I check my watch for the fifth time in as many minutes. The training room fills with paramedics and EMTs chatting about calls and complaining about paperwork, but I barely register their conversations. My eyes keep drifting to the door.

"Someone's jumpy today," Dani slides into the seat next to me, coffee in hand. "You're not usually this anxious about continuing education credits."

"Just caffeinated," I lie, tapping my empty travel mug.

"Right." She doesn't believe me for a second. "Nothing to do with a certain doctor who's teaching this session?"

Heat creeps up my neck. "It's been a week since coffee. We've texted but—"

The door opens and Liam walks in, dressed in dark slacks and a light blue button-down that makes his eyes look impossibly clear. My sentence dies mid-thought.

"But you haven't seen him," Dani finishes for me, smirking. "Got it."

Liam sets his materials on the table at the front of the room. He looks up, scanning the faces until his eyes lock with mine. A small, private smile touches his lips before he shifts into professional mode.

"Good morning, everyone. Thanks for coming to today's session on advanced airway management techniques." His voice carries confidence, but I catch the slight adjustment of his collar—a nervous tell I somehow recognize despite our limited time together.

The first thirty minutes pass in a blur of slides and discussion. I contribute when appropriate, but mostly I watch him. The way his hands move when he explains complex procedures. How he listens intently to questions, head slightly tilted. The occasional glance my way that lasts a beat longer than necessary.

"Now we'll move on to the practical portion," Liam announces. "I need a volunteer to demonstrate the new bougie-assisted cricothyrotomy technique we're implementing."

Several hands go up. Mine isn't one of them—I'm too busy trying to look professional while my heart pounds against my ribs.

"Paramedic Bennet," Liam says, his eyes finding mine. "You've had experience with difficult airways, correct?"

"Yes, Doctor." My voice comes out steadier than I feel.

"Perfect. Would you mind helping with the demonstration?"

I rise from my chair, aware of Dani's knowing look as I pass. Walking to the front of the room feels like crossing a football field.

"The patient presents with severe facial trauma and upper airway obstruction," Liam explains to the room as I position myself by the training mannequin. "Standard intubation attempts have failed."

He stands close enough that I catch his scent—antiseptic soap and something warmer underneath, something distinctly him. Our fingers brush as he hands me a pair of gloves.

"You'll assist while I demonstrate," he says, his voice pitched for the room but his eyes communicating something else entirely.

I nod, not trusting my voice.

"First, identify the cricothyroid membrane," Liam explains, turning toward me. "May I?"

I nod again. His fingers touch my neck, gentle but precise. The contact sends electricity through my body.

"You'll palpate here," he continues, his fingertips pressing lightly against my throat. His professional demeanor doesn't falter, but his pulse—visible at his wrist—quickens. "Feel for the depression between the thyroid cartilage and cricoid ring."

The room full of people fades away. There's only the point of contact between us, warm and charged with something beyond medical instruction.

"Your hands need to be steady," Liam says, his voice dropping slightly. "Even when the situation is intense."

Our eyes meet. A silent acknowledgment passes between us.

He clears his throat and turns back to the mannequin. "Now I'll demonstrate the actual procedure."

I hand him instruments before he asks, anticipating each need. We move in perfect synchrony, like we've worked together for years instead of days. The rest of the class watches, but I feel the weight of their attention differently now—wondering if they can see what's happening between us.

"Perfect assist, Paramedic Bennet," Liam says when we finish. "That's exactly the kind of teamwork that saves lives in the field."

As the class breaks into practice groups, Liam leans closer. "You knew exactly what I needed before I asked."

"It keeps happening," I murmur. "Like I've done this with you a thousand times."

"I know." His voice is low, meant only for me. "It's getting harder to ignore."

"Do we want to ignore it?" I ask, aware of colleagues nearby but unable to stop myself.

"No." The single word carries weight. "But this isn't the place to discuss it."

For the remainder of the session, we maintain professional distance. I work with my group, demonstrating techniques Liam just taught. But awareness of his presence follows me like a shadow—I know exactly where he stands in the room without looking.

As people file out at the end, I deliberately pack my bag slowly. Dani passes with a whispered "Text me later" and a knowing wink.

When the room empties, Liam approaches my table. "You're a natural teacher," he says. "Your group had the best technique."

"I had a good instructor today." I zip my bag closed but don't move to leave.

"Noah." The way he says my name makes my chest tighten. "This thing between us…"

"Is getting stronger," I finish.

He nods, running a hand through his hair. "A week of texting, and I still couldn't prepare myself for seeing you today."

"When you touched my neck—" I start.

"I know." His eyes darken slightly. "Everyone was watching, but all I could think about was—"

The door opens and a nurse pokes her head in. "Dr. Winters? Dr. Kapoor is looking for you."

Liam straightens, the professional mask sliding back into place. "Tell her I'll be right there."

The door closes, leaving us in suspended animation.

"We need to talk," I say. "Really talk about this."

"Dinner?" he suggests. "Tonight? My shift ends at eight."

"I'll pick you up at the staff entrance." I shoulder my bag, fighting the urge to touch him. "Eight-fifteen."

He nods, a smile playing at the corner of his mouth. "I'll be there."

Chapter 5

Liam

I check my watch for the third time in two minutes. 7:58 PM. Noah isn't late—I'm early. Again. The hospital staff exit doors hiss behind me as another nurse leaves, nodding goodbye.

My fingers smooth down my wrinkled scrubs. I'd planned to change before our dinner, but a last-minute consult with an elderly patient stretched longer than expected. Now I'm standing here in the same blue scrubs I've worn for the past twelve hours, feeling distinctly underdressed for what my brain keeps labeling as a "date" despite my attempts to downplay it.

The exit door opens again, and Noah steps out. His dark hair is slightly damp, freshly washed, and he's changed into dark jeans and a forest green button-down that makes his eyes look impossibly deeper. My stomach does a strange little flip.

"Hey," he says, smiling as he approaches. "You made it."

"Barely." I gesture at my scrubs with an apologetic grimace. "Sorry about... this. Mrs. Abernathy had questions about her husband's medication changes, and before I knew it—"

"You look great." Noah's eyes travel down my body in a way that makes my pulse quicken. "Actually, those scrubs showcase your ass quite nicely."

Heat rushes to my face, but I laugh, tension draining from my shoulders. "Medical school never prepared me for that particular professional assessment."

"Consider it my expert paramedic opinion." His grin is infectious. "So, I know a place a few blocks from here. Nothing fancy, but the food's good."

"Lead the way."

We fall into step beside each other, our shoulders occasionally brushing as we navigate the evening sidewalk traffic. The contact, brief as it is, sends little sparks across my skin each time.

"Rough shift?" Noah asks.

"Not terrible. Mostly routine cases, though we had a nasty tibia fracture come in right before lunch. You?"

"Three cardiac calls, one false alarm, and an elderly woman who just wanted someone to check her blood pressure because she didn't trust her home monitor."

"And did you?"

"Check it? Of course. It was perfect—120/80 on the dot. I think she was just lonely."

Something in his voice—that natural compassion that seems to radiate from him—warms me from within. "That's... really kind of you."

"It's part of the job." Noah shrugs, but I catch the hint of a smile.

The diner Noah leads us to is a retro-style place with neon signs and vinyl booths. A bell chimes as we enter, and a waitress with a name tag reading "Doris" waves us to a booth by the window.

"My regular spot," Noah explains as we slide in opposite each other. "They make the best milkshakes in the city."

"You're a milkshake connoisseur?"

"Among my many talents." He winks, and my stomach does that flip again.

Doris brings us menus and water, greeting Noah by name. After she leaves, I raise an eyebrow.

"So you bring all your dates here?"

The question slips out before I can filter it, but Noah doesn't miss a beat.

"Only the special ones." His eyes hold mine. "And for the record, this is the first time I've brought anyone from work here."

I take a sip of water to hide whatever my face might be revealing. "I'm honored."

"You should be. Their burgers are legendary."

Conversation flows easier than I expected as we order and wait for our food. Noah tells me about growing up with three sisters in a small town outside the city, and I share stories about my medical school disasters.

"Wait—you actually sutured your pants to the practice dummy?" Noah's laugh fills the space between us.

"In my defense, it was hour thirty-six of a forty-eight hour shift. I'm lucky I didn't sew my hand to it."

Our food arrives—burgers and fries for both of us, with the promised milkshakes—and the conversation continues without a pause. I find myself relaxing more with each passing minute, the awkwardness I'd feared nowhere to be found.

I'm halfway through my burger when Noah sets down his milkshake and gives me a curious look.

"So what's your long-term plan, Dr. Winters? Still going to be running the ER in five years? Ten?"

The question catches me off guard. I carefully set my burger down, wiping my fingers on a napkin to buy myself a moment.

"Honestly? I don't know." I meet his eyes, finding no judgment there, just genuine interest. "After everything with Jason, I was so focused on just... rebuilding. Getting through each day. Making a new life here." I shrug, feeling oddly vulnerable. "I haven't really thought much beyond that."

"That makes sense," Noah says, nodding. "Sometimes you need to heal before you can plan."

"Exactly. I threw myself into work because it was the one thing that made sense when everything else didn't." I trace a pattern in the condensation on my water glass. "What about you? Always wanted to be a paramedic supervisor?"

"Not specifically. I just knew I wanted to help people, to make a difference. After my brother..." He pauses, and I remember the story he shared about losing his brother. "I just needed to be part of preventing other families from experiencing that kind of loss."

I nod, understanding completely.

Noah leans forward slightly, his expression shifting to something more playful. "So this future you haven't planned yet—think there might be room in it for a milkshake connoisseur with excellent taste in diners?"

My heart skips a beat. The directness of his question both thrills and terrifies me. But looking at him across the table, I find myself wanting to be honest.

"I think," I say carefully, "that I'd be very open to that possibility."

Noah's smile grows wider, and he reaches across the table. His fingers brush against mine, sending electricity up my arm. I don't pull away.

"Good to know," he murmurs.

The diner's ambient noise seems to fade as we lean toward each other, the space between us charged with possibility. Noah's eyes drop to my lips, and I find myself mirroring him, wondering what he tastes like. Probably vanilla milkshake with a hint of—

A sharp, strangled gasp from the booth behind us shatters the moment. I turn to see a young girl, maybe eight or nine, clutching at her throat, her face rapidly reddening.

"Emily?" A woman's panicked voice rises. "Emily, what's wrong?"

Noah and I are on our feet simultaneously.

"Ma'am, I'm a paramedic and this is a doctor," Noah says, his voice instantly shifting to professional calm. "What happened?"

"I don't know! She was eating her ice cream and then—" The mother's eyes widen in horror. "Oh God, there must have been peanuts. She's allergic to peanuts!"

I'm already assessing the child. Facial swelling, labored breathing, hives appearing on her neck. Classic anaphylaxis.

"Do you have an EpiPen?" I ask, checking the girl's pulse—rapid and thready.

"In my purse, but we just used her last one last month and I haven't—" The mother's voice breaks.

Noah's already pulling out his phone. "I'm calling 911. We need an ambulance."

I look around the diner. "Does anyone have an EpiPen? This child is having a severe allergic reaction!"

The diner falls silent, faces blank or shaking heads. The girl's breathing becomes more labored, a wheeze audible now.

"Noah, we can't wait. Metropolitan General is four blocks away. We need to move her now."

He nods, already ending his call. "My car's right outside, I left it here early when I came to meet you."

I turn to the mother. "Ma'am, we need to get your daughter to the hospital immediately. She's having a severe allergic reaction."

She nods frantically, gathering her purse as Noah gently lifts the girl. Her lips are starting to turn blue.

"Keep her upright," I instruct as we rush toward the door, leaving cash thrown hastily on the table.

Noah's car is parked in a loading zone just outside. He places the girl in the backseat, and I slide in beside her, the mother following. Noah jumps in the driver's seat and peels away from the curb.

"Emily, stay with me," I say, monitoring her pulse and respiratory effort. "We're getting you help."

Noah drives with the precision of someone used to emergency situations, taking corners fast but smoothly. He catches my eye in the rearview mirror. "Two minutes out. How is she?"

"Respiratory distress increasing. Stridor present." I support her in a sitting position, watching her struggle for each breath. "Faster, Noah."

He pushes the car harder, and true to his word, we screech to a halt at the emergency entrance exactly two minutes later. Noah's out of the car before I can even reach for the door handle, already shouting for help.

"Nine-year-old female, anaphylactic shock, no EpiPen administered!"

Dr. Chen appears at the entrance, summoned by Noah's shouts, and helps transfer the girl to a waiting gurney. I follow them in, giving rapid-fire information as we move.

"Symptoms began approximately seven minutes ago. Suspected peanut exposure. Progressive respiratory distress, facial edema, urticaria."

Chen nods, already calling for epinephrine as we wheel the girl into Trauma 1. Noah and I step back as the ER team takes over, administering the medication that will save her life.

The mother stands beside us, trembling. "Is she going to be okay?"

"The team is giving her epinephrine now," I explain. "It works very quickly. Her breathing should improve within minutes."

True to my word, within moments of receiving the injection, Emily's breathing eases. The monitors show her heart rate beginning to normalize. The crisis is passing.

Noah and I exchange a look of relief, and I suddenly realize how close we're standing, his shoulder pressed against mine. His hand finds mine and squeezes briefly.

"Nice teamwork, Dr. Winters," he says softly.

"You too, Supervisor Bennet."

We watch as Emily continues to improve, color returning to her face. The moment in the diner—that almost-kiss—hangs between us, unacknowledged but not forgotten.

"Rain check on that milkshake?" Noah asks, his voice low enough that only I can hear.

I meet his eyes, finding them filled with the same mixture of adrenaline and attraction I'm feeling.

"Definitely."

Act 2

Chapter 6

Liam

I glance at the monitor displaying the vitals of the elderly man I've just admitted for pneumonia. His oxygen saturation has improved since we started him on the antibiotics and supplemental oxygen, but my thoughts aren't fully on Mr. Garrison's respiratory rate.

"BP's stable at 132/78," Nurse Keisha reports, updating the chart. "Fever's down to 100.2."

"Good. Let's continue the current treatment plan and reassess in four hours." I sign off on the orders, but my pen hovers over the chart longer than necessary.

Last night keeps replaying in my mind. Noah sitting across from me in that vinyl booth, the way the diner's neon lights caught the angles of his face. The moment when he leaned forward, his eyes dropping to my lips, and I knew—I knew—he was going to kiss me.

"Dr. Winters?" Keisha's voice breaks through my thoughts. "You've been signing that chart for about thirty seconds now."

I blink, realizing I've been staring blankly at the page. "Sorry. Just... double-checking the dosage."

She gives me a knowing look. "Mmhmm. I'm sure that's what has you looking like you're a million miles away."

I clear my throat and close the chart with more force than necessary. "What's next?"

"Abdominal pain in Exam 3, chest pain in 5, and your favorite—a toe laceration in 2."

"Let's start with the chest pain." I reach for the next chart, but my mind immediately drifts back to Noah.

The way we moved together last night during Emily's emergency—no words needed, just that inexplicable synchronicity. His hands steady as he drove, his voice calm as he called out to the ED staff. Then that brief moment when his fingers found mine in the chaos, a small squeeze that felt more intimate than any kiss could have been.

I shake my head, trying to focus as I enter Exam 5. Mrs. Patel, 62, with three hours of substernal chest pain radiating to her left arm. I need to be present for this. Lives depend on my attention.

"Mrs. Patel, I'm Dr. Winters. Can you tell me about your chest pain?"

I go through the motions—asking about her symptoms, ordering an ECG and cardiac enzymes, listening to her heart and lungs. My hands perform the examination with practiced precision, but behind my professional facade, I'm remembering Noah's voice: "Rain check on that milkshake?"

Two hours later, I've cleared half the board. Mrs. Patel's troponin was negative, and her ECG showed no acute changes. The abdominal pain turned out to be constipation, and the toe laceration needed only three stitches. It's the kind of shift I usually appreciate—busy enough to be interesting but not overwhelming.

Yet I can't stop thinking about Noah. About what might have happened if Emily hadn't had her allergic reaction. Would I have let him kiss me? Would I have kissed him back?

Of course I would have. I've been drawn to him since that first trauma case we worked together. There's something about him that feels like... home. Like I've known him forever.

"Earth to Liam." Mira appears beside me at the nurses' station, coffee in hand. "This is your second time reading the same lab result."

I sigh, setting down the paper. "That obvious, huh?"

"Only to someone who's known you for years." She leans against the counter. "Let me guess—tall, blond paramedic supervisor?"

"We almost kissed last night."

Her eyebrows shoot up. "Almost?"

"We were at Bernie's Diner, and right when it was about to happen, a kid at the next table had an anaphylactic reaction."

"Only you two would have your first kiss interrupted by a medical emergency." She laughs softly. "So what happens now?"

"I don't know." I run a hand through my hair. "We said we'd reschedule, but..."

"But you're overthinking it already." Mira gives me a gentle nudge. "Classic Liam Winters move."

She's right. I'm already cataloging all the ways this could go wrong. What if this connection we feel is just adrenaline and proximity? What if he's not ready for something serious? What if I'm not? After Jason, I swore I'd focus on my career, avoid the complications of dating another medical professional.

But Noah isn't Jason. That much I know for certain.

I'm reviewing discharge paperwork when the overhead page blares through the emergency department.

"Attention all staff, Code Orange. Multiple casualty incident. ETA for first ambulances, three minutes."

My body shifts into emergency mode before my mind can fully process the announcement. Code Orange—mass casualty incident. The controlled chaos begins immediately, nurses clearing beds, techs readying equipment, residents looking to attendings for direction.

Dr. Kapoor appears beside me. "Construction site collapse downtown. Early reports suggest at least fifteen injured, multiple critical."

I nod, already mentally triaging resources. "Let's clear trauma bays one through four. Move the stable patients to the hallway if necessary."

The first ambulances arrive in a parade of flashing lights and wailing sirens. I stand at the ambulance bay doors, ready to direct traffic. The first two patients have minor injuries—lacerations and a possible broken arm. The third ambulance brings a woman with a crush injury to her lower extremities.

Then I hear it—the distinctive siren of Medic 17. Noah's rig.

The ambulance backs in with precision, and the rear doors fly open. Noah jumps out first, his face set in concentration, hands steady on the gurney.

"Male, 42, construction worker. Fell fifteen feet onto rebar. Impaled through the right flank. The bar is still in place. Vitals stable for now but he's getting tachy. We've stabilized the bar as best we could for transport."

Our eyes lock for a split second, and something electric passes between us. Then we're moving.

"Trauma One," I direct, falling into step beside the gurney.

The patient—Ted, according to his hard hat—is awake and terrified. A steel reinforcement bar about two inches in diameter protrudes from his right side, just below the ribcage. Blood seeps slowly around the entry point, but it's the internal damage I'm worried about.

"Ted, I'm Dr. Winters. We're going to take care of you."

"Am I gonna die?" His voice shakes, eyes wide with fear.

"Not if I have anything to say about it," I assure him as we transfer him to the trauma bed. "Try not to move. That bar is acting like a plug right now."

Noah positions himself at the head of the bed, speaking softly to Ted while connecting him to our monitors. I don't need to tell him what to do—he's already placed himself perfectly to keep the patient calm and still.

The trauma team swarms around us—nurses, techs, a surgical resident. I call for immediate portable X-ray and ultrasound, and blood products on standby.

"BP dropping, 100/60," a nurse calls out.

I perform a rapid assessment. The bar has entered laterally through the right flank, and based on the angle and depth, it's likely perilously close to the iliac artery. One wrong move could nick it, causing catastrophic bleeding.

"We need OR, now," I say, examining the imaging as soon as it appears on the screen. The ultrasound confirms my fear—the bar is millimeters from the major vessel.

"OR 3 is prepping, but they're still ten minutes out," the charge nurse reports.

Ted groans, shifting slightly on the bed. The monitors immediately respond—his heart rate jumps to 120.

"We can't wait," I decide. "We need to stabilize this bar better before transport or he won't make it to the OR."

Noah meets my eyes across the patient. "The vibrations from moving him could shift it."

I nod. "Exactly."

Without another word, Noah reaches for the sterile packing material I hadn't even asked for yet. As I carefully examine the entry wound, he's already opening packages, preparing gauze soaked in hemostatic agent.

"I need a better view of the entry point," I murmur, and Noah immediately adjusts the overhead light, then gently shifts Ted's arm to give me better access, all while maintaining perfect steadiness around the impaled object.

The trauma resident steps forward. "Should I call for thoracic consult?"

"No time," I reply, not looking up. "We need to create a stabilizing structure around this bar before transport."

Noah hands me exactly what I need before I can ask—a modified pressure dressing designed to immobilize the bar while supporting the surrounding tissue. As I work to secure it, Noah prepares the next component.

"We'll need to build a protective frame," I say.

Noah is already fashioning one using supplies from the trauma cart. "Like this?" He holds up a structure created from splinting materials.

"Perfect."

The room has grown quiet except for the beeping monitors and our focused exchanges. I become aware that the other trauma team members have paused to watch us work. Dr. Chen stands in the doorway, her expression a mixture of awe and confusion.

Working in tandem, Noah and I secure the bar with a combination of specialized dressings and the improvised stabilization frame. Our hands move in perfect synchronization—when I reach for tape, he's cutting it; when I need to adjust Ted's position slightly, Noah is already supporting the critical areas.

"Heart rate normalizing," the nurse reports. "BP coming back up, 110/70."

"Good," I nod. "Let's get him to OR now. This will hold for transport."

As we prepare to move, Ted reaches up and grabs my wrist. "Doc, I don't know what just happened, but thank you."

"You're going to be fine, Ted. The surgeons will remove that bar safely now."

As the team wheels him toward the elevator, unexpected applause breaks out among the staff who had gathered to watch. Dr. Kapoor gives an approving nod.

Noah and I stand side by side, suddenly aware of everyone's eyes on us.

"That was..." Dr. Chen starts, shaking her head slightly. "I've never seen anything like that coordination before."

I feel Noah's presence beside me, steady and warm. Neither of us responds to Chen's implied question.

"The patient's stable for surgery," I say instead, stripping off my gloves. "That's what matters."

***

Noah

The surgical team wheels Ted away, his vitals finally stable after our frantic work to save him. The rebar that had impaled him now removed, the bleeding controlled. I exhale deeply, only now realizing I'd been holding my breath. My scrubs cling to my back, soaked with sweat from the intensity of the trauma response.

Liam stands beside me, his surgical gown splattered with blood. He pulls off his gloves with a snap and tosses them into the biohazard bin. Even exhausted, hair plastered to his forehead, he looks beautiful to me.

"Break room?" he suggests, voice hoarse.

I nod, following him through the organized chaos of the ED. We pass nurses and techs cleaning up the trauma bay, restocking supplies, preparing for the next emergency that will inevitably arrive. The rhythm of the hospital continues around us, but for a moment, we step outside the current.

The break room is mercifully empty. Liam collapses onto the worn couch against the wall, head tilted back, eyes closed. I grab two bottles of water from the mini-fridge and join him, our shoulders touching as I sink into the cushions.

"Here." I offer him the water.

His fingers brush mine as he takes it. "Thanks."

We drink in silence for a minute, letting the adrenaline ebb from our systems. My body feels heavy, but my mind is crystal clear—hyperaware of Liam's proximity, the rise and fall of his chest, the faint scent of his cologne beneath the antiseptic hospital smell.

"We saved him," I say finally, rolling the cool bottle between my palms.

Liam turns his head toward me, a tired smile playing at his lips. "We did."

"That feeling never gets old, does it? Pulling someone back from the edge."

"Never." Liam shifts, angling his body toward mine. "That moment when you know they're going to make it... it's why I do this."

"Me too." I look down at my hands, remembering the weight of the instruments as we worked to free Ted from the rebar. "After my brother died, I spent years feeling helpless. But days like today—"

"They make it worth it," Liam finishes.

I meet his eyes. "Exactly."

"It's different with you there," he admits quietly. "When we're working together, I feel... I don't know how to describe it."

"Invincible," I offer. "Like we can't fail."

His eyes soften. "Yes."

The door swings open, and we both straighten reflexively. Dr. Eleanor Hayes, Chief of Surgery, walks in, her commanding presence filling the small room. Her silver-streaked dark hair is pulled back in a tight bun, her expression serious but not stern.

"Dr. Winters. Mr. Bennet." She nods to each of us. "I just came from observing the beginning of Mr. Crawford's surgery."

Liam sits up straighter. "How's he doing?"

"Stable, thanks to your work in the ED." Dr. Hayes crosses her arms, regarding us both. "Dr. Chen told me about your coordination during the initial assessment. Said he's never seen anything like it."

I feel heat rise to my cheeks. "We just did what needed to be done."

"No," she counters, "you did more than that. That patient had a mortality prediction of over eighty percent when he came through those doors. The surgical team is optimistic he'll make a full recovery."

Liam's hand finds mine between us on the couch, hidden from Dr. Hayes's view. His fingers interlace with mine, squeezing gently.

"The trauma response was textbook perfect," Dr. Hayes continues. "The speed and precision with which you stabilized that impalement injury... frankly, it was impressive."

"Thank you," Liam says. "Noah's expertise was invaluable."

Dr. Hayes's sharp eyes move between us. "Whatever you two have going on—this partnership—it works. I've been in medicine for thirty years, and I recognize exceptional teamwork when I see it." She pauses. "Don't lose that."

With a final nod, she turns and leaves, the door swinging shut behind her.

Liam's hand is still in mine. I look down at our intertwined fingers, then back up to his face.

"She noticed it too," I murmur.

"Everyone notices it." Liam doesn't pull his hand away. "I've never experienced anything like this before. Not with any colleague, not with anyone."

"Me neither." I take a breath, gathering courage. "It scares me sometimes. How right it feels to work with you. Like we've done this a thousand times before."

"I know." His thumb traces circles on the back of my hand. "When that rebar shifted, and you knew exactly how to stabilize it before I even said anything—"

"Or when you called for the thoracotomy tray three seconds before I was about to ask for it—"

We both laugh softly, the shared understanding hanging between us.

"It feels good," Liam says after a moment. "Not just saving lives, but... doing it together." His voice drops lower. "Being with you makes everything clearer somehow."

I lean closer, drawn to him like gravity. "I feel the same way."

His eyes drop to my lips, then back up. The moment stretches between us, electric with possibility.

"I don't want to mess this up," he whispers. "Whatever this is."

"We won't," I promise, though I have no right to make such guarantees. But in this moment, with his hand in mine and the shared triumph of saving a life together still thrumming through us, I believe it.

Chapter 7

Noah

I study Liam's profile as we sit side by side, the energy between us humming like a live wire. The break room feels both too small and too vast all at once. His hand in mine anchors me to this moment— this impossible, perfect moment.

"So," I say, my voice lower than intended. "About that dinner we never quite finished..."

Liam's eyes meet mine, curiosity dancing in them. "What about it?"

"I was thinking maybe we could try again." I run my thumb across his knuckles, savoring the simple contact. "But this time, let me cook for you."

His eyebrows lift slightly. "You cook?"

"Don't sound so surprised." I laugh, nudging his shoulder with mine. "I'm actually pretty good. My grandmother was Italian—she wouldn't let any of her grandchildren leave home without knowing how to make a proper meal."

"Is that so?" A smile plays at the corners of his mouth. "And what would you make for me, Noah Bennet?"

The way he says my full name sends a pleasant shiver through me. "That depends. What do you like?"

"Surprise me." His eyes never leave mine, and there's something in them—a vulnerability, an openness—that makes my heart beat faster.

"Challenge accepted." I squeeze his hand gently. "Tonight? Say, eight o'clock?"

Liam hesitates, and for a moment I worry he's going to say no. Then he nods, and the smile that breaks across his face is breathtaking.

"Eight sounds perfect." He glances at our still-intertwined hands. "I should probably finish my shift without thinking about this all afternoon, but..."

"But you will anyway?" I finish for him.

"Yeah." He laughs softly. "I will."

We reluctantly separate our hands as the sounds of the hospital filter back into our awareness. The moment feels fragile, precious—like something I need to protect.

"I'll text you my address, drop by after you're done" Liam says, standing up. He stretches, and I catch a glimpse of skin where his scrub top lifts. "Try not to save any more lives before then. I don't think my heart can take another adrenaline rush today."

I stand too, close enough that I can feel the heat radiating from him. "No promises. Saving lives is kind of our thing."

"Our thing," he repeats, eyes softening. "I like the sound of that."

He's so close I can see the faint stubble on his jaw, count the flecks of gold in his irises. The urge to kiss him right here, consequences be damned, is almost overwhelming.

"Eight o'clock," I remind him, my voice rough. "Don't stand me up, Dr. Winters."

"Wouldn't dream of it." His gaze drops briefly to my lips before he takes a deliberate step back. "I should get back to the ED."

I nod, not trusting myself to speak. As he reaches the door, he turns back, that same unguarded expression on his face.

"Noah?"

"Yeah?"

"I'm looking forward to it." The simple honesty in his voice makes my chest tight.

"Me too."

After he leaves, I sink back onto the couch, letting out a long breath. My hand still tingles where his fingers had been interlaced with mine. Eight o'clock suddenly feels very far away.

I pull out my phone, already mentally planning the menu. Something impressive but not pretentious. Something that shows I care without trying too hard. Something that might—just might—be worthy of the way Liam Winters looks at me when he thinks I don't notice.

My grandmother's carbonara recipe. Fresh pasta if I can manage the time. A good bottle of wine. Simple, authentic food that speaks for itself.

I text my roommate to make himself scarce tonight, then head back to the ambulance bay, unable to keep the smile off my face. For the first time in years, I feel something I'd almost forgotten: anticipation, pure and sweet, for what comes next.

* * *

Noah

I'm chopping garlic with perhaps more concentration than the task requires when the doorbell rings. My knife freezes mid-slice as my heart does a strange little flip in my chest.

"He's here," I mutter to myself, quickly wiping my hands on a kitchen towel.

I take a deep breath before opening the door. Liam stands in the hallway, dressed in dark jeans and a soft-looking blue sweater that makes his eyes seem even more intense than usual. He's holding a bottle of wine and looks about as nervous as I feel.

"Hey," I say, suddenly aware of my own casual outfit—jeans and a henley with the sleeves pushed up.

"Hey yourself." He offers the wine, a small smile playing at his lips. "I wasn't sure what you were making, so I brought both red and white."

"Perfect timing. I was just starting the carbonara." I step aside to let him in, catching a hint of his cologne as he passes. "Make yourself at home."

My apartment isn't anything special—open concept living room and kitchen, decent-sized windows, mismatched furniture I've collected over the years—but I spent the afternoon making sure it was spotless. Liam glances around, taking it all in.

"I like your place," he says, setting the wine on the counter. "It feels lived-in. Like a home."

"Thanks." I return to my cutting board, strangely self-conscious. "My roommate's out for the night, so it's just us."

Liam nods, lingering at the edge of the kitchen. "Can I help with any-thing?"

"You're the guest," I protest, but he's already rolling up his sleeves.

"I'm not much of a cook, but I can follow instructions." He washes his hands at the sink, standing close enough that our elbows brush. "What are we making?"

"Carbonara. My grandmother's recipe." I slide a bowl of eggs toward him. "Think you can handle whisking these with some grated pecorino?"

He takes the bowl with a determined expression. "I believe in my whisk-ing abilities."

As I return to the garlic, I feel some of my nervousness dissipate. There's something about having him in my kitchen, sleeves pushed up and focused on his task, that feels unexpectedly right.

I start explaining the recipe as I work. "The trick is to have everything ready before the pasta's done. Once the pasta comes out of the water, we need to move fast."

Liam nods, whisking with surprising skill. "So it's all about timing."

"Exactly." I smile, reaching for the pancetta. "Can you grab that pepper grinder?"

Before I can point to it, Liam's already handing it to me. Our fingers brush, and I look up in surprise.

"How did you know which one I meant?"

He shrugs, looking equally puzzled. "I don't know. I just... knew."

I turn back to the stove, a strange warmth spreading through me that has nothing to do with the heat of the burner. As I start cooking the pancetta, Liam moves around me to grab a wooden spoon—exactly the one I was about to reach for.

"This is what you need, right?" he asks, handing it to me.

I nod slowly. "Yeah, it is."

Over the next twenty minutes, we fall into a rhythm that feels impossi-ble for two people who've never cooked together before. Liam hands me ingredients before I ask, adjusts the heat when I'm thinking it needs to be lower, and somehow knows exactly when to drain the pasta—right when I'm about to tell him it's time.

When I need more space to work, he steps back. When I need help, he's there. Not once do we bump into each other or get in each other's way.

"This is weird, right?" I finally say as we're plating the pasta. "The way we're moving around each other?"

Liam looks up, relief washing over his face. "Oh thank god, you feel it too. I thought I was imagining things."

"It's like…" I search for the right words. "It's like you know what I'm going to do before I do it."

"Or like I can hear what you're thinking." He sets down the tongs, focusing fully on me now. "Noah, this isn't normal."

"No," I agree, leaning against the counter. "It's not. But it's not just in the hospital. It's here too."

Liam runs a hand through his hair, messing it up in a way that makes him look younger, less guarded. "I've never experienced anything like this before. With anyone."

"Me neither." I hesitate, then decide to just be honest. "In my past relationships, I was always the one doing all the work. Trying to anticipate what they needed, bending over backwards to make things smooth. But with you…"

"With me?"

"With you, it's effortless. Like we're two parts of the same system." I gesture between us. "You don't just take. You give back. You participate. Even when we're just making pasta."

Something softens in his expression. He steps closer, close enough that I can see the different shades of blue in his eyes.

"I feel it too," he says quietly. "Like we're in sync in a way that shouldn't be possible."

I don't know what to say to that, so I just hold his gaze, letting the truth of it settle between us. Whatever this connection is—this impossible, inexplicable thing—it's real. And it's ours.

"The pasta's getting cold," I finally say, though food is the last thing on my mind.

Liam smiles, and the simple beauty of it catches me off guard. "Then we should eat."

I set our plates on the small dining table by the window, where I've lit a couple of candles. Nothing too fancy—I didn't want to seem like I was trying too hard—but the soft light makes everything feel more intimate.

"This looks amazing," Liam says, taking a seat.

"Let's hope it tastes as good as it looks." I pour us each a glass of the white wine he brought. "My nonna would disown me if I ruined her recipe."

Liam twirls pasta around his fork and takes a bite. His eyes close briefly, and a small smile forms on his lips. "If she disowns you, I'll adopt you. This is incredible."

I laugh, relief washing through me. "High praise from someone who claims he can't cook."

"I never said I couldn't eat." He takes another bite. "Seriously, this is the best carbonara I've had outside of Italy."

"You've been to Italy?" I ask, genuinely curious.

"Med school graduation gift to myself. Two weeks eating my way through Rome, Florence, and Naples." His expression turns sheepish. "I actually took a cooking class in Rome, but the only thing I retained was how to drink wine properly."

"Show me," I challenge.

He demonstrates an elaborate ritual of swirling, sniffing, and sipping that has me laughing so hard I nearly choke on my pasta.

"What about you?" he asks after I've recovered. "Worst boss you've ever had?"

I groan, setting down my fork. "Oh god, that's easy. My first paramedic supervisor, Harrison. He was this old-school guy who thought EMS was still all about 'scoop and run.' No interventions in the field, just get them to the hospital as fast as possible."

"Those guys are the worst," Liam agrees, refilling our glasses. "We had an attending like that when I was a resident. Dr. Critchner. He'd yell if you ordered any test that wasn't absolutely necessary."

"What did he consider necessary?"

"Basically nothing." Liam rolls his eyes. "One time I ordered a head CT for a patient with the worst headache of their life and new neurological symptoms. Critchner ripped into me for wasting resources."

"Let me guess—the patient had a bleed?"

"Subarachnoid hemorrhage," Liam confirms. "When the results came back, Critchner just grunted and walked away. No apology, no acknowledgment that I'd made the right call."

"Sounds like Harrison. Once I gave epinephrine to an anaphylaxis patient before getting online medical control, and he wrote me up for exceeding my scope of practice." I shake my head at the memory. "The patient would have died if I'd waited."

"What happened?"

"The medical director—not you, your predecessor—tore up the write-up and told Harrison to take a refresher course on the protocols." I grin. "Harrison avoided me for months after that."

As we eat, the conversation flows easily between us. I tell him about the time I got locked in the hospital morgue during my EMT training, and he counters with a story about accidentally setting off the fire alarm during a med school practical exam.

"You did not," I say, laughing.

"I absolutely did." He's laughing too, his eyes crinkling at the corners. "I was so nervous I knocked over a Bunsen burner. The entire class had to evacuate, and we all had to retake the exam the next day."

"Did you pass?"

"With flying colors. Turns out near-death experiences are great for test anxiety."

I learn that Liam was pre-med at McGill before medical school at University of Toronto, that he has a younger sister who teaches elementary school, and that he's allergic to cats but had three growing up anyway.

Liam glances at our empty plates and smiles. "That was incredible. Let me help clean up."

We clear the table together, moving around each other with that same strange synchronicity we've had since the beginning. I wash while he dries, and we fall into an easy rhythm, our shoulders occasionally brushing as we work.

"You know," I say, handing him a clean plate, "I still can't get over how easy this is."

"What? Doing dishes?" He takes the plate, his fingers brushing mine.

"Being with you." I turn off the water and face him fully. "It's like I've known you forever."

He sets down the dish towel, his eyes meeting mine. "I know what you mean."

Something shifts in the air between us. I step closer, drawn by an invisible pull I couldn't resist even if I wanted to. Liam doesn't back away. If anything, he leans in slightly, his gaze dropping to my lips.

In one fluid motion, I place my hands on his waist and lift him onto the counter. His eyes widen in surprise, but before he can say anything, I lean in and press my lips against his.

For a heartbeat, he's still. Then his arms wrap around my neck, pulling me closer as he deepens the kiss. His lips are soft but insistent, and I feel a current running through me, electric and alive.

I step between his legs, my hands finding their way to his back, holding him against me as the kiss intensifies. He tastes like wine and something uniquely him, and I'm already addicted.

Liam's fingers thread through my hair as our kiss deepens, sending shivers across my scalp. I pull back just enough to look at him—his flushed cheeks, his slightly parted lips, the dazed look in his eyes. Something inside me clicks into place, like the final piece of a puzzle I didn't know I was solving.

"Come here," I whisper, taking his hand and gently helping him down from the counter.

I lead him to the living room, our fingers intertwined. When we reach the couch, he pulls me down beside him, immediately leaning in to recapture my lips. His hand finds my jaw, thumb brushing against my cheek with unexpected tenderness.

"I've been wanting to do this since I first saw you," I confess against his mouth.

He smiles, the warmth of it spreading through me. "Even covered in blood in trauma one?"

"Especially then." I press a kiss to the corner of his mouth. "You were so focused, so in control. It was incredibly hot."

He laughs softly, the sound vibrating against my lips. "You have strange turn-ons, Bennet."

"You have no idea," I murmur, leaning in again.

This time when we kiss, it's slower, more deliberate. I take my time exploring the shape of his mouth, the taste of him. His hand slides down my neck to my chest, resting over my heart, which pounds beneath his palm. I ease him back against the cushions, half-covering his body with mine as the kiss deepens.

His hands find their way under the hem of my shirt, cool fingers tracing patterns on the small of my back. The touch sends a jolt through me, and I respond by nipping gently at his lower lip. He makes a soft sound in the back of his throat that nearly undoes me.

I pull back just enough to look at him, taking in his disheveled hair and the intense blue of his eyes. "Is this okay?" I ask, suddenly aware of how quickly things are escalating.

"More than okay," he breathes, pulling me back down to him.

We lose track of time, trading kisses that range from achingly gentle to breathlessly urgent. My hand finds its way beneath his sweater, tracing the warm skin of his side, feeling the slight ridge of his ribs beneath my fingertips. He arches into the touch, his own hands growing bolder as they explore my back, my shoulders, the nape of my neck.

When we finally separate, we're both breathing hard. Liam's sweater is rumpled, his hair a mess from my fingers. I'm sure I look equally disheveled, but I couldn't care less. All I can focus on is the way he's looking at me—like I'm something precious and unexpected.

"That was..." he starts, then shakes his head, seemingly at a loss for words.

"Yeah," I agree, understanding completely.

I shift to sit beside him rather than on top of him, though I keep one hand on his knee, not quite ready to break contact. He reaches for my other hand, lacing our fingers together.

"So," he says after a moment, "that happened."

I laugh, squeezing his hand. "It did. And I'd very much like it to happen again."

His expression turns serious, though his eyes remain warm. "Noah, we should talk about what this means. For us, for work."

I nod, sobering. "You're right."

"I'm your medical director," he says, stating the obvious but necessary point. "There are... complications."

"I know." I run my thumb across his knuckles. "But I also know that what's happening between us isn't something I want to walk away from."

He looks down at our joined hands. "Me neither. Which scares me a little, if I'm being honest."

"Because of Jason?" I ask gently.

He nods. "Partly. But also because of how quickly this is moving. How intense it feels already."

"I feel it too." I take a deep breath. "Look, I'm not suggesting we announce this to the hospital tomorrow. In fact, I think we should keep this between us for now."

"You do?" He looks surprised.

"Absolutely. This is new, and it's ours. I don't want everyone at Metro

General weighing in with their opinions before we've even figured out what 'this' is." I gesture between us. "Plus, there's the whole chain of command thing to consider."

Relief washes over his face. "I was thinking the same thing. We should be discreet, at least until we're sure about where this is going."

"And we need to be professional at work," I add. "No making out in supply closets, tempting as that might be."

He laughs, the tension breaking. "Agreed. Though now that you've mentioned it..."

I grin, leaning in to press a quick kiss to his lips. "Save that thought for after hours, Dr. Winters."

He smiles against my mouth. "I'm serious about this, Noah. About us. I want to see where this goes."

"So am I," I assure him, pulling back to meet his gaze. "I don't know what this connection between us is—this weird mind-reading thing—but I know it's part of something bigger. Something worth exploring."

He nods, his expression softening. "So we're doing this? Dating? Secretly?"

"Dating," I confirm, liking the sound of it. "Exclusively, I hope?"

"Definitely exclusively." He squeezes my hand. "And yes, secretly. For now."

I lean my forehead against his, closing my eyes. "I can work with that."

We stay like that for a moment, sharing the same breath, the same space. Despite the complications, despite the need for discretion, I feel a certainty I've rarely experienced before. Whatever this is between us—this inexplicable connection, this immediate understanding—it's real. And it's worth protecting.

Chapter 8

Liam

I push through Metropolitan General's sliding doors, a strange weightlessness in my step that hasn't been there in years. My lips still tingle from Noah's kiss last night. The memory of his hands on my waist, his mouth against mine, floods my body with heat that has nothing to do with the hospital's overactive heating system.

The usual morning chaos of the emergency department swirls around me—monitors beeping, staff calling out to each other, the squeak of gurney wheels on linoleum—but it all seems distant, like background noise to the symphony playing in my head. A symphony composed entirely of Noah Bennet.

"Morning, Dr. Winters." Nurse Martinez hands me a tablet. "Bed three needs discharge papers, and we've got abdominal pain in five waiting on labs."

"Thanks." I take the tablet, trying to force my mind into work mode. "Anything critical?"

"Not yet, but give it time." She narrows her eyes. "You look... different today."

I clear my throat. "New scrubs."

"Same scrubs you always wear." Her lips curl into a knowing smile. "But something's definitely new."

Heat crawls up my neck as I turn away, pretending to study the patient board. Maintaining professional discretion about Noah and me is going to be harder than I thought if I can't even control my own face.

In the doctors' lounge, I grab my white coat and stethoscope from my locker. My phone buzzes with a text.

Morning, Dr. Gorgeous. Can't stop thinking about last night.

My stomach flips like I'm back in high school with my first crush. This is ridiculous. I'm a 34-year-old emergency physician who's handled everything from mass casualties to telling families their loved ones didn't make it. Yet here I am, grinning at my phone like an idiot because a paramedic called me gorgeous.

Not just any paramedic. Noah. The man who somehow knows what I'm thinking before I do. The man whose touch sparked something in me I thought had died with Jason's betrayal.

Focus on your patients. Some of us have actual work to do. I text back, then add: *But last night was perfect.*

Three dots appear immediately. *You're perfect. Dinner at your place tonight?*

Yes. Now go save lives.

I slip my phone into my pocket, aware that I should feel alarmed by how quickly this is all happening. Noah and I have known each other for what—a few weeks? And already we're exclusive, already I'm counting the hours until I can see him again. By all logical reasoning, I should be terrified.

Instead, I feel alive. Like I've been sleepwalking through life and Noah's kiss woke me up.

"Dr. Winters, got a minute?" Dr. Chen appears at my side, startling me out of my thoughts.

"Of course." I follow her to a computer terminal, where she pulls up a CT scan.

"Fifty-eight-year-old male with intermittent abdominal pain for three days. Look at this."

I study the scan, forcing my brain to switch gears. "Small bowel obstruction. Probably adhesions from his previous surgeries."

"That's what I thought. Surgery's on their way down."

As we discuss the treatment plan, my mind keeps drifting to Noah's apartment, to the way he pressed me against his kitchen counter, his mouth hot on my neck, his hands sliding under my shirt—

"Liam?" Chen waves her hand in front of my face. "You still with me?"

"Sorry. Yes. Call me when surgery arrives."

She gives me a curious look. "Everything okay? You seem... distracted."

"Just thinking about a complex case." The lie comes easily, but guilt follows. Chen deserves better than my divided attention.

"Right." She doesn't look convinced. "By the way, that construction worker with the rebar impalement? He's being discharged to rehab today. Remarkable recovery."

"That's great news."

"The OR nurses are still talking about how you and that paramedic supervisor worked together. What was his name again?"

"Noah Bennet." His name feels intimate on my tongue, like a secret.

"That's it. Hayes says he's never seen anything like it. You two had some kind of mind-meld thing going on."

I try to keep my expression neutral. "We work well together."

"Uh-huh." Chen's pager beeps. "Saved by the bell. But this conversation isn't over, Winters. Something's up with you, and I'm going to figure it out."

As she walks away, I exhale slowly. This is going to be harder than I thought.

In trauma one, I examine a college student with a dislocated shoulder from a skateboarding accident. My hands move through the familiar assessment, but my mind keeps replaying moments from last night—Noah's laugh as we cooked together, the taste of wine on his lips, the way his body felt pressed against mine.

"This might hurt," I warn the patient as I prepare to reduce his shoulder.

The procedure is quick and successful, but afterward, I duck into an empty exam room to collect myself. What is happening to me? I've never been this distracted at work, not even during the worst of the Jason debacle.

But this isn't like Jason. With Jason, there was always a performance aspect—both of us playing the roles of brilliant, ambitious doctors building a power couple. With Noah, there's none of that pretense. Just this inexplicable connection that feels both brand new and ancient, like we've known each other across lifetimes.

My pager beeps with a trauma alert. As I hurry toward the ambulance bay, I wonder if Noah will be bringing in this patient. The thought sends another rush of anticipation through me that I quickly tamp down. I need to compartmentalize. When I'm at work, I'm Dr. Winters first, Liam second.

Even if all I can think about is the way Noah's hands felt on my skin, and how many hours until I can feel them there again.

* * *

Noah

I can't wipe this stupid grin off my face as I walk into the station. The morning sun feels different today—brighter, more alive—just like everything else since Liam and I started... whatever this is between us.

Dani's already at her locker, checking inventory on her jump bag when I stroll in whistling.

"Well, well, well." She stops what she's doing, zipping up the bag with a dramatic flourish. "Someone got laid last night."

"Good morning to you too, Daniela." I open my locker, still smiling despite her bluntness.

"Seriously, Bennet. You're practically glowing. It's disgusting." She leans against the lockers, arms crossed. "So who's the lucky guy?"

I hesitate, glancing around the locker room. We're alone, and if there's anyone I trust with this information, it's Dani. She's been my partner for two years and knows how to keep a secret.

"If I tell you something, you have to swear it stays between us."

Her eyes widen. "Oh my god, it's someone I know?"

"Dani."

"Fine, fine. I swear on my grandmother's grave."

"Your grandmother is still alive."

"Then I'll have to kill her, because I need to know this gossip."

I can't help but laugh. "It's Liam. Dr. Winters."

For a second, she just stares at me. Then she erupts.

"WHAT?!" She squeals so loudly I have to clap my hand over her mouth. She swats it away. "DR. HOT STUFF WINTERS? ARE YOU KIDDING ME?!"

"Jesus, Dani, the whole department's going to hear you!"

She starts bouncing up and down, grabbing my shoulders. "Oh my god, oh my god, oh my god! The ice king himself? How did this happen? When did this happen? I need every single detail right now!"

I can't help but laugh at her reaction. "It just... happened. We've been feeling this connection since we first worked together."

"That weird thing where you finish each other's medical procedures? I've seen it! Everyone's seen it!" She gasps dramatically. "Wait, is he good in bed? He seems like he'd be really... thorough. Her eyebrows waggle suggestively as she pronounces the last word."

"Dani!"

"What? It's a legitimate question!" She's practically vibrating with excitement. "Oh my god, when's the wedding? Can I be your best woman? I call dibs!"

I shake my head, feeling my cheeks heat up. "We haven't even slept together yet, not that it's any of your business."

She stops bouncing, her jaw dropping. "Why the hell not? You've been making goo-goo eyes at each other for weeks!"

I close my locker, leaning against it as I try to find the right words. "We're taking things slow. Everything else between us has happened so fast, this weird connection, the way we work together... it just didn't feel right to rush this part."

My mind drifts back to last night—Liam's lips on mine, the way his hands felt against my skin, how perfectly we fit together. "When it happens, I want it to be because we're both ready, not because we got caught up in the moment."

Dani's expression softens. "Look at you, all grown up and having mature relationships." She punches my arm lightly. "I'm happy for you, Noah. Seriously."

"Thanks." I glance at the clock. "We should get going. Rig check in five."

"Fine, but this conversation isn't over." She points a finger at me as we head toward the bay. "I want updates. Regular updates."

"You're worse than my mother."

"Your mother doesn't know you're dating the hottest doctor at Metro Gen."

I laugh, but the sound catches in my throat as I realize something. "Hey, Dani?"

"Yeah?"

"I think I might be falling in love with him."

The words surprise even me, but as soon as they're out, I know they're true. It's terrifying and exhilarating all at once.

Dani stops walking and turns to face me, all teasing gone from her expression. "Wow. You're serious."

"I know it's fast, but there's something about him, Dani. Something I can't explain. When we're together, it's like I've known him my entire life."

She studies my face for a moment, then nods. "Then don't screw it up, Bennet." She smiles and loops her arm through mine as we continue walking. "And for what it's worth, I've seen the way he looks at you when he thinks no one's watching. I think the feeling might be mutual."

I feel that stupid grin spreading across my face again. "You really think so?"

"God, you're hopeless." She laughs. "Come on, Romeo. Let's go save some lives while you daydream about your doctor boyfriend."

As we head to the ambulance bay, I check my phone one last time. There's a new message from Liam:

Miss you already. Be safe out there today.

I type back quickly: *Always. Can't wait to see you later.*

"You're doing it again," Dani says, watching me.

"Doing what?"

"That face. Like you just won the lottery."

I tuck my phone away, still smiling. "Maybe I did."

* * *

Liam

I stare at the disaster zone that used to be my kitchen. Smoke curls from a pot of what was supposed to be risotto but now resembles concrete. The cutting board displays a massacre of unevenly chopped vegetables. My phone timer blares for the third time, reminding me about whatever I've forgotten in the oven.

"Shit, shit, shit." I grab a dishcloth and yank open the oven door. A plume of smoke hits my face as I extract the charred remains of garlic bread. The smoke detector shrieks in protest.

Why did I think I could cook? Medical school taught me to save lives, not prepare edible food. I've subsisted on takeout and hospital cafeteria meals for years. But something about Noah made me want to impress him with a home-cooked meal after he prepared that incredible carbonara.

The doorbell rings.

"No, no, no. He's early." I check my watch—he's actually right on time. I'm just hopelessly behind schedule.

I hurry to the door, dishcloth still in hand, my blue button-down shirt splattered with what might be tomato sauce or possibly blood. At this point, either seems plausible.

Noah stands in the hallway, a bottle of wine in one hand and a small bouquet of flowers in the other. His smile fades as he takes in my frazzled appearance and the smoke wafting from behind me.

"Are you under attack in there?" His eyes crinkle with amusement.

"The kitchen definitely declared war." I step aside to let him in. "I may have overestimated my culinary abilities."

Noah follows me into the apartment, his eyebrows rising as he surveys the kitchen carnage. He sets down his gifts and walks to the stove, lifting the lid on my failed risotto. "What was this supposed to be?"

"Don't laugh."

"I'm not laughing." But his lips twitch traitorously.

"You're absolutely laughing."

He breaks into a full grin. "Maybe a little. But it's cute. You're cute when you're flustered."

Heat rises to my face that has nothing to do with the smoking oven. "I wanted to make you dinner. You know, reciprocate after your amazing carbonara."

Noah's expression softens. He steps closer, brushing a smudge of flour from my cheek. "I appreciate the effort. Really."

"The effort that's going to leave us ordering takeout?"

"Not necessarily." Noah rolls up his sleeves. "Let's see what we can salvage."

"Noah, you don't have to—"

"I want to." He moves around my kitchen with the same confidence he shows in trauma situations. "What were you planning to make?"

"Risotto with pan-seared chicken and roasted vegetables. Ambitious, I know."

"We can work with that." Noah opens my refrigerator. "You've got the ingredients, at least."

I watch as he assesses the situation, mentally triaging my culinary disaster the way we would approach multiple trauma patients.

"The vegetables are fine—just need proper seasoning. The chicken hasn't been touched yet. And we'll start fresh with the risotto." He looks at me. "Cooking is like medicine—it's all about timing and technique."

Something warm unfurls in my chest as Noah hands me a fresh cutting board. "Here. Cube the chicken while I prep a new batch of risotto."

We fall into a rhythm that feels strangely familiar. I finish with the chicken just as Noah needs it. He stirs the risotto while instructing me on how to season the vegetables. Our movements around the small kitchen space become a synchronized dance—he steps left as I move right, I reach for the salt just as he's finished with it.

"How do you know exactly what I'm going to do?" I ask, noticing how he's already holding out the olive oil before I've even reached for it.

"Same way I know which instrument you need during a procedure before you ask." Noah shrugs. "I can't explain it. I just... feel what you're thinking."

Working together, we transform the chaos into something approaching order. The risotto simmers properly this time, creamy and aromatic. The chicken sizzles in the pan, and the vegetables roast in the oven.

"Taste this." Noah holds out a spoon of risotto.

I lean forward, my eyes locked on his as I taste. "Perfect."

"See? We make a good team."

Thirty minutes later, we're seated at my rarely-used dining table, plates of surprisingly delicious food before us. I've lit candles—the one decorative touch I managed before everything went sideways—and Noah's flowers sit in a water glass because I don't own a proper vase.

"To teamwork," Noah raises his wine glass.

"To saving dinner." I clink my glass against his. "And thank you. For not running away when you saw the state of things."

"Are you kidding? I like seeing this side of you—the imperfect, human side. Dr. Winters isn't always in control after all."

"Only around you, it seems." I take a bite of the risotto. "This is incredible."

"We made it together." Noah reaches across the table, his fingers brushing mine. "That's what made it work."

After dinner, we migrate to the sofa with our wine glasses. Noah scrolls through my streaming options.

"You have a collection of old movies?" He sounds delighted.

"A weakness for classic cinema. Especially the romantic ones."

"Roman Holiday?" Noah suggests.

"Perfect."

As Audrey Hepburn and Gregory Peck fall in love against the backdrop of Rome, Noah's arm slides around my shoulders. I lean into him, feeling more at home in my own apartment than I have in years.

When he turns to kiss me, it's soft and unhurried. His hand cups my face, thumb tracing my cheekbone with a gentleness that makes my chest ache.

"This is nice," he murmurs against my lips.

"Better than nice." I pull him closer, tasting wine and possibility on his tongue.

On screen, Audrey and Gregory share an ice cream. On my sofa, Noah and I share something I'm starting to believe might be far more significant than either of us anticipated.

I find myself sinking deeper into Noah's embrace as the movie plays on. His arm feels perfectly weighted around my shoulders, like it was designed to rest there. Our hands have found each other, fingers intertwined in the space between us on the couch. Every so often, his thumb traces small circles on my skin, sending pleasant shivers up my arm.

"I've always loved this scene," I murmur as Audrey Hepburn's character experiences the freedom of zooming through Rome on a Vespa.

Noah's lips brush against my temple. "Is that why you became a doctor instead of a princess? No royal scooter budget?"

I laugh, the sound bubbling up naturally. "You caught me. My entire career path determined by insufficient Vespa funding."

He pulls me closer, and I rest my head against his shoulder. The solid warmth of him feels like an anchor, keeping me present in this moment rather than drifting into thoughts of tomorrow's patients or yesterday's mistakes.

As the movie progresses toward its bittersweet ending, I find myself paying less attention to the screen and more to the steady rise and fall of Noah's chest, the way his heartbeat feels against my cheek when I turn my head just so.

When the credits roll, neither of us moves immediately. The spell of the evening feels too precious to break.

"I should probably get going," Noah says finally, though he makes no effort to disentangle himself from me.

My heart races as I consider what I want to say next. The words feel vulnerable in my mouth, but I push them out anyway.

"You could stay. If you want to."

Noah shifts slightly to look at me. "Stay?"

"Just to sleep," I clarify quickly, feeling heat rise to my face. "I'm not suggesting—I mean, not that I don't want to eventually, but—"

He silences my rambling with a gentle kiss. "I'd love to stay."

The simple acceptance in his voice loosens something tight in my chest. "Yeah?"

"Yeah." His smile is soft in the dim light. "Nothing would make me happier than waking up next to you."

We move through my apartment with a comfortable domesticity that should feel strange given how new this is, but somehow doesn't. I lend him a T-shirt and sweatpants that hang a little loose on his frame.

In the bathroom, I open the cabinet beneath the sink and pull out a new toothbrush still in its packaging—blue to match my green one.

"Here," I say, handing it to him. "This can be yours. For whenever you're here."

Noah takes the toothbrush, looking at it with an expression that seems disproportionate to such a simple item. "You're giving me drawer space already, Dr. Winters?"

There's teasing in his voice, but something else too—a tender recognition of what this small gesture means.

"Just bathroom counter space for now," I reply, trying to keep my tone light despite the significance humming between us. "Drawer space is at least three more dates away."

"I'll work my way up to closet space," he promises with a wink.

We brush our teeth side by side, catching each other's eyes in the mirror and smiling around foam-filled mouths like teenagers. It's ridiculous and perfect.

In my bedroom, I feel a momentary flash of self-consciousness as Noah takes in the space—the meticulously made bed with its navy duvet, the stacks of medical journals on the nightstand, the distinct absence of personal touches that might make it feel truly lived in.

"Which side do you sleep on?" he asks.

"Left."

"Perfect. I'm a right-side sleeper."

Of course we're compatible even in this. I switch off the overhead light, leaving just the soft glow of my bedside lamp. We slide under the covers, and there's a brief, awkward shuffle as we figure out how our bodies fit together in this new context.

Then Noah's arm comes around my waist, pulling me against him, my back to his chest. The tension in my shoulders melts away as he tucks me against him, his breath warm against the nape of my neck.

"This okay?" he murmurs.

"More than okay."

I feel safe in a way I haven't in years—maybe ever. It's not just physical safety; it's the emotional security of being held by someone who seems to understand me on a level I can't rationally explain.

"Tell me something I don't know about you yet," Noah says into the quiet darkness.

I think for a moment. "I wanted to be a veterinarian until I was fourteen and had to put my dog down. I decided then that I'd rather work with patients who could tell me where it hurts."

His arm tightens around me. "What was your dog's name?"

"Galileo. Gali for short. He was a golden retriever mix."

"I bet he was a good boy."

"The best." I smile into the darkness. "Your turn."

Noah's voice rumbles against my back. "I can't whistle. Not even a little bit. It's my greatest shame."

I laugh, turning slightly in his arms. "Really? That's your deep dark secret?"

"I've tried everything. My brother could whistle the entire theme to Star Wars. I can't even get a single note."

"That's adorable."

"It's embarrassing is what it is," he protests, but I can hear the smile in his voice.

We continue like this, trading small revelations—how I'm terrified of heights but love roller coasters, how he once ate nothing but peanut butter sandwiches for an entire month as a child, how we both cry at commercials involving rescue animals.

I don't remember falling asleep. One moment I'm listening to Noah's soft voice describing his grandmother's garden, and the next I'm drifting, wrapped in warmth and the certainty that I'm exactly where I'm supposed to be.

Chapter 9

Liam

I can't stop smiling as I review Mrs. Houlihan's chart at the nurses' station. The numbers and notes blur slightly as my mind drifts back to this morning—the gentle weight of Noah's arm draped across my chest, the soft press of his lips against my shoulder blade waking me just before my alarm.

"Someone's in a good mood," Nurse Garcia comments as she passes by, eyebrow raised.

I school my expression into something more professionally neutral. "Just a good night's sleep."

It wasn't a lie. I slept better with Noah beside me than I have in months, maybe years. There was something about his steady breathing, the solid warmth of him, that quieted the usual parade of patient concerns and administrative worries that typically march through my mind.

"Uh-huh." She doesn't look convinced but mercifully doesn't press further.

I turn my attention back to Mrs. Houlihan's labs, forcing myself to focus. Her white count is trending down, good response to the antibiotics. I make a note to decrease her IV fluids and consider oral medications if she continues to improve.

But my mind keeps circling back to Noah.

This morning, he'd propped himself up on one elbow, watching me with sleepy eyes as I moved around my bedroom gathering clothes for the day. "You're beautiful," he'd murmured, voice rough with sleep.

I'd felt my cheeks warm at the compliment, unused to being observed so openly, so appreciatively. "You need glasses."

"My vision is perfect, thank you very much. Twenty-twenty in both eyes."

When I emerged from the shower with just a towel around my waist, I caught him politely averting his gaze, a gesture so unexpectedly gentlemanly it made my heart constrict. He wasn't pushing, wasn't assuming anything—just respecting boundaries neither of us had explicitly discussed yet.

"You can look, you know," I'd told him, feeling bold and vulnerable all at once.

His eyes had met mine, a slow smile spreading across his face. "Just trying to be respectful. But if you're offering..."

The memory of his appreciative gaze as I dressed makes me warm even now, standing in the clinical fluorescence of the ED.

"Dr. Winters?" A voice pulls me from my reverie. It's Dr. Chen, looking at me expectantly. "The CT results for bed three?"

"Right, yes." I clear my throat, embarrassed to be caught daydreaming. "No evidence of intracranial hemorrhage. We can discharge with concussion protocol and follow-up instructions."

Dr. Chen nods, but gives me a curious look. "You okay? You seem distracted."

"I'm fine. Just... thinking through a complex case."

My phone vibrates in my pocket, and I resist the urge to check it immediately. I finish reviewing orders with Chen, consult on a new admission with atypical chest pain, and check on a child with a forearm fracture before I finally have a moment to slip into the medication room for privacy.

The message is from Noah, and my heart does a ridiculous little flip when I see his name on my screen.

Thanks for last night. Is it bad that I never want to sleep anywhere else again?

I lean against the shelves, grinning like an idiot at my phone. The medication room door opens, and I quickly pocket my phone, pretending to be searching for something on the shelf.

"Looking for something, Dr. Winters?" It's Mira, giving me a knowing look.

"Just, uh, checking our supply of... amiodarone."

She glances at the clearly labeled cardiac medication shelf on the opposite wall. "Over there, but nice try." She lowers her voice. "Your face is flushed. Either you're coming down with something, or that was a message from a certain paramedic supervisor."

I sigh, knowing there's no point denying it to Mira. "We had dinner at my place last night."

"And breakfast this morning?" Her eyes dance with amusement.

"Nothing happened," I say quickly. "I mean, not nothing, but not... we just slept. Together. Sleep-slept."

"And that has you looking like you just won the lottery because...?"

I can't help the smile that breaks through again. "It was nice. Really nice."

Mira squeezes my arm. "I'm happy for you, Liam. Truly."

When she leaves, I pull out my phone again and type a reply to Noah:

If that's bad, I don't want to be good. My bed already feels empty without you.

I hesitate, wondering if that's too much, too soon. But it's the truth. I hit send before I can overthink it.

His response comes almost immediately:

Tonight? My place? I'll make breakfast this time.

I type back: *I'm off at 8. I'll bring dessert.*

Three dots appear, then: *You ARE dessert.*

I nearly drop my phone, heat rushing to my face. Before I can respond, the trauma alert sounds overhead. I pocket my phone, take a deep breath to center myself, and head toward the trauma bay—still smiling, still feeling like I'm floating just slightly above the ground.

* * *

I'm in the middle of updating a patient's chart when Dr. Lawrence Hadley, the hospital's general medical director, appears beside me. His presence is always imposing—tall, silver-haired, with the kind of authoritative demeanor that commands attention without effort.

"Dr. Winters, do you have a moment?"

"Of course," I say, closing the chart and giving him my full attention.

"Let's step into my office." His tone is measured but serious enough to make my stomach tighten.

We walk in silence to the administrative wing. Dr. Hadley's office is spacious, with windows overlooking the hospital grounds and walls lined with medical texts and framed credentials. He gestures for me to take a seat across from his desk.

"We've received a formal complaint against one of the paramedic crews," he begins, sliding a folder across his desk. "As ED Medical Director and liaison to EMS, I need you to investigate."

I open the folder and scan the first page. My blood runs cold when I see the name: Noah Bennet, Paramedic Supervisor.

"The patient, Mrs. Eleanor Grimes, alleges that the paramedic crew was dismissive of her symptoms, made inappropriate comments about her weight affecting their ability to transfer her, and delayed care while arguing about treatment protocols." Dr. Hadley folds his hands on the desk. "She specifically named Supervisor Bennet as being, quote, 'arrogant and negligent.'"

I struggle to keep my expression neutral. "I see."

"I understand you've been working closely with Bennet on the protocol revisions. I trust that won't affect your ability to conduct an impartial investigation?"

My throat feels dry. "Of course not."

If he only knew how close Noah and I have become. If he knew I'd woken up in Noah's arms just this morning. If he knew I could feel Noah's heartbeat against my back as he whispered about how much he looked forward to seeing me tonight.

"Good. I'll need your report by Friday. Interview all parties involved, review the run reports and any relevant medical records." He stands, signaling the end of our meeting. "The hospital takes these complaints seriously, Dr. Winters. I expect thoroughness."

"Understood."

Back in the ED, I find an empty consultation room and close the door. I read through the complaint again, more carefully this time. Mrs. Grimes, 72, had called 911 with chest pain. According to her statement, the paramedics—Noah and his partner Dani—had made comments suggesting her symptoms were probably indigestion due to her weight. She claimed they delayed transport while arguing about whether her EKG showed concerning changes, and that Noah had been dismissive when she expressed fear about having a heart attack.

This doesn't sound like Noah at all. I've seen him with patients—he's compassionate, attentive, professional. He treats everyone with dignity.

But I'm hardly objective, am I?

I pull out my phone, tempted to text Noah about this immediately, but stop myself. This is an official investigation now. Contacting him outside proper channels would compromise the process.

God, what a mess. I'm literally dating the person I'm supposed to be investigating. I have access to his personal life, his thoughts, his character in ways no investigator should. I know in my heart Noah wouldn't treat a patient the way Mrs. Grimes described. But is that knowledge or bias speaking?

I put the folder away and try to focus on my remaining patients, but my mind keeps circling back to the complaint. By the time my shift ends, I've constructed and discarded a dozen approaches to handling this situation.

As I'm changing in the locker room, my phone buzzes with a text from Noah:

Just got home. Can't wait to see you. Should I start dinner or wait for you?

I stare at the message, guilt and conflict churning in my stomach. How do I respond? Do I cancel? Do I pretend everything's fine and then blindside him with an official interview tomorrow?

Neither option feels right.

I type back: *Something's come up. Can I call you in a few minutes?*

His response is immediate: *Of course. Everything okay?*

I finish changing and head to my car. Once inside, I take a deep breath and call him.

"Hey," Noah answers, his voice warm. "What's going on?"

"Noah, I..." I pause, struggling to find the right words. "Dr. Hadley gave me an assignment today. A complaint was filed against a paramedic crew, and I'm supposed to investigate."

There's a moment of silence. "Okay. And?"

"It's your crew, Noah. You and Dani. From a call two days ago. Mrs. Grimes?"

"Mrs. Grimes?" I hear the confusion in his voice. "The chest pain call? What did she complain about?"

"She's claiming you were dismissive of her symptoms, made inappropriate comments about her weight, and delayed care while arguing about protocols."

"What?" The shock in his voice sounds genuine. "Liam, that's not—we never—"

"I know," I say quickly. "At least, I think I know. But that's the problem, Noah. I'm supposed to be impartial here, and I'm... not. I'm dating you. I care about you. I'm inherently biased."

Noah is quiet for a moment. "So what are you saying?"

"I don't know." I run a hand through my hair. "I'm conflicted. I should probably recuse myself, but then I'd have to explain why, and we agreed to keep things discreet for now. But if I don't, and I find in your favor—which I believe I would, because I don't think you'd ever do what she's claiming—it could look like I wasn't thorough or objective."

"This is a mess," Noah says softly.

"Yeah." I lean my head back against the seat. "I don't know what to do."

I sit in my car for a long moment after ending the call with Noah, my head spinning with conflicting thoughts. The parking garage's fluorescent lights cast harsh shadows across the dashboard as I grip the steering wheel, trying to center myself.

This isn't right. I can't investigate Noah impartially—not when I know the gentle way he touches my face when he thinks I'm asleep, not when I've felt his heartbeat quicken against my palm, not when I've seen firsthand how he treats every patient with dignity regardless of their condition.

My phone buzzes with a text from Noah: *Should I still expect you tonight?*

I type back: *Rain check? I need to figure some things out first.*

His response is immediate: *I understand. Let me know if you need anything.*

Even now, he's putting my needs first. How could I possibly conduct an unbiased investigation?

The next morning, I arrive at the hospital early and head straight to Dr. Hadley's office. His assistant isn't at her desk yet, but his door is open. He's already reviewing charts, reading glasses perched on the end of his nose.

"Dr. Winters," he looks up, surprised. "Early bird today?"

"I need to speak with you about the Grimes complaint," I say, standing in his doorway.

"Come in." He gestures to the chair across from him. "Have you already made progress?"

I take a seat and straighten my shoulders. "I need to recuse myself from the investigation."

His eyebrows rise. "That's unusual. May I ask why?"

"I have a personal relationship with Supervisor Bennet that would compromise my objectivity." The words come out more steadily than I expected.

Dr. Hadley removes his glasses, studying me with new interest. "I see. And what is the nature of this relationship?"

"We're dating." Saying it aloud in this context makes my heart race. "It's relatively new, but serious enough that I can't in good conscience conduct this investigation."

He nods slowly. "I appreciate your honesty, Dr. Winters. Professional integrity is paramount in situations like this."

"I'd recommend Dr. Kapoor handle the investigation instead," I suggest. "She has experience with EMS oversight and no personal connections to the paramedic staff."

"That's a reasonable suggestion." He makes a note on his legal pad. "I assume you understand this disclosure has implications beyond just this investigation?"

"Yes. We've been discreet because of the supervisory aspects of my role with EMS, but we were planning to disclose the relationship formally soon." This isn't entirely true, but it feels right saying it.

"You'll need to file the appropriate paperwork with HR. There will need to be adjustments to the reporting structure for Supervisor Bennet." His tone is matter-of-fact, not judgmental. "Dr. Chen could take over the direct oversight of his unit to avoid conflicts of interest."

"I understand."

Dr. Hadley puts his glasses back on. "For what it's worth, Dr. Winters, I've observed Supervisor Bennet's work. He's exemplary. This complaint surprised me as well."

Relief washes through me. "Thank you for understanding."

"Thank you for your integrity. I'll speak with Dr. Kapoor this morning."

I leave his office feeling lighter despite the uncertainty ahead. I text Noah: Can you meet me at the coffee shop across from the hospital in 30 minutes?

His reply comes quickly: I'll be there.

The coffee shop is quiet at this hour. I grab a table in the corner and order an Americano, watching the door. When Noah walks in, my heart does that familiar skip. He's wearing his uniform pants and a navy department polo, hair slightly damp like he rushed through his morning shower.

He spots me and walks over, concern etched across his face. "Hey."

"Hey," I reply as he sits across from me. "Thanks for coming."

"Of course." He reaches for my hand but stops himself, remembering we're in public. "Did you figure things out?"

"I recused myself from the investigation this morning," I tell him. "I spoke with Dr. Hadley and told him about us."

Noah's eyes widen. "You did?"

"I couldn't investigate you, Noah. It wouldn't be right—for the hospital, for Mrs. Grimes, or for us." I wrap my hands around my coffee cup. "I can't pretend to be objective about someone I care about this much."

His expression softens. "What did Hadley say?"

"He was surprisingly understanding. Dr. Kapoor will handle the investigation instead." I take a deep breath. "But this means we can't hide anymore. We need to file paperwork with HR, and Dr. Chen will take over supervision of your unit."

Noah nods slowly, processing this. "So everyone will know about us."

"Is that okay?" I ask, suddenly uncertain. "I know we agreed to keep things discreet, but—"

"It's more than okay," he interrupts, his voice firm. "I've wanted to tell everyone since our first date. I just didn't want to complicate things for you professionally."

Relief floods through me. "Really?"

"Liam, I'm falling in love with you," he says, his voice low but clear. "I don't want to hide that."

My heart stutters at his words. This is the first time either of us has used the word "love."

"I'm falling in love with you too," I admit, the truth of it settling comfortably in my chest.

Noah smiles, that bright, open smile that first caught my attention. "Then I'd say this complaint, as frustrating as it is, might have done us a favor."

"How do you figure?"

"It forced us to stop hiding." He reaches across the table, no longer hesitating, and takes my hand. "And I'm really tired of pretending I don't light up every time I see you."

I squeeze his hand, feeling a weight lift off my shoulders. Whatever comes next—the investigation, the HR meetings, the hospital gossip—we'll face it together, in the open.

Chapter 10

Liam

I feel the stares as I walk down the hallway toward the nurses' station. Two medical assistants lean close together, whispering, then abruptly stop when they notice me approaching. Their smiles are too bright, too knowing.

"Good morning, Dr. Winters," they say in near-unison.

"Morning," I reply, keeping my voice neutral as I reach for the tablet to check my patient list.

It's been three days since Noah and I filed our relationship disclosure with HR, and word has spread through Metropolitan General faster than a norovirus outbreak. I've faced four trauma cases, diagnosed two rare conditions, and saved countless lives in this hospital, yet now I'm primarily known as "the doctor dating the hot paramedic supervisor."

Mira slides up beside me at the computer station, coffee in hand. "You're the talk of the break room again," she says, not bothering to hide her amusement.

"Wonderful," I mutter, scrolling through lab results. "Don't people have actual work to do?"

"Oh, we do. But multitasking is a nursing superpower." She sips her coffee. "Besides, it's good gossip. Two impossibly attractive emergency medicine professionals finding love amid the chaos? It's practically a romance novel."

I shoot her a glare. "We're not characters in a book."

"The nurses in Cardiology have a betting pool on when you'll move in together," she continues, ignoring my irritation. "And Radiology thinks you're already engaged but keeping it secret."

"We've been dating for a few weeks!"

"True love waits for no one, Liam." She pats my arm sympathetically. "If it helps, it's all very positive gossip. Everyone thinks you're adorable together."

Before I can respond, my phone buzzes with a text from Noah: *Incoming trauma, 5 minutes. 42-year-old male, construction accident, partial amputation of left arm.*

I pocket my phone and grab my stethoscope. "Trauma incoming. Partial arm amputation."

Mira nods, immediately shifting to professional mode. "I'll set up Trauma One."

When Noah's ambulance arrives, I'm waiting with the trauma team. The doors swing open, and there he is, focused and professional as he rattles off vital signs and intervention details. Our eyes meet briefly, and despite the critical situation, I feel that familiar flutter.

"Patient maintained consciousness throughout transport," Noah reports as we transfer the man to the trauma bay. "We've got the amputated limb here in cooling. Vascular access established, one liter of saline infused."

"Good work," I say, already examining the patient. "Let's get two units of O-neg hanging, call vascular and plastics for consult."

Noah and his partner step back as my team takes over, but he lingers at the edge of the room, completing his paperwork. I'm acutely aware of his presence as I work, even with my back turned.

When the patient is stabilized and headed to surgery, Noah approaches me in the hallway.

"Hey," he says softly.

"Hey yourself," I reply, unable to stop the smile that forms. "Good save out there."

"The cooling protocol for the limb—that was something you mentioned in the training last month. Thought you'd appreciate seeing it implemented."

"I did." Our conversation is professional, but I notice three nurses at the station pretending not to watch us while failing spectacularly at the attempt.

Noah notices too and lowers his voice. "Is it my imagination, or are we being observed like rare specimens in a zoo?"

"It's not your imagination," I sigh. "Apparently, we're the hottest gossip in the hospital. There are betting pools."

His eyebrows shoot up. "Betting pools? About what?"

"When we're moving in together. Or getting engaged. Take your pick."

Noah laughs, the sound warm and rich. "Well, that's... flattering? I think?"

"It's ridiculous," I mutter, though I can't help but smile at his reaction.

"Dr. Winters!" Dr. Chen calls from down the hall, waving a tablet. "Need your input on a case."

"Duty calls," I tell Noah. "See you later?"

"Count on it." He brushes his fingers against mine briefly—the smallest touch, but enough to send electricity through me.

As I walk toward Dr. Chen, I hear giggles behind me. Two nurses are watching, one whispering to the other, "They're so cute together."

I pretend not to hear, but feel heat rising to my cheeks.

Later that afternoon, I'm reviewing charts when Noah appears with two coffee cups.

"Thought you might need this," he says, setting one beside me. "Double shot, splash of cream, no sugar."

"You're a lifesaver," I say gratefully, taking a sip. "How'd you know I was crashing?"

"Just had a feeling." He leans against the counter. "Plus, you always get that little crease between your eyebrows around hour ten of your shift."

"I do not," I protest, even as I consciously try to relax my forehead.

"You absolutely do." His smile is teasing. "It's adorable."

From the corner of my eye, I spot two medical assistants nudging each other and looking our way.

"We have an audience again," I murmur.

Noah follows my gaze and sighs. "You know, I've been shot at, trapped in burning buildings, and dangled from a helicopter during a rescue, but somehow this feels more unnerving."

"The great Noah Bennet, intimidated by hospital gossip?" I tease.

"Not intimidated. Just... adjusting." He takes a sip of his own coffee. "I'm used to being professional Noah at work. This is new territory."

"I know what you mean." I lower my voice. "I've spent years building my reputation here as Dr. Winters, not Liam who gets googly-eyed over the paramedic supervisor."

"Googly-eyed, huh?" His grin widens.

"You know what I mean," I say, fighting a smile.

A group of nurses walks by, one of them audibly whispering, "They're so perfect together, it's almost annoying."

Noah and I exchange looks and burst into laughter.

"Maybe we should just embrace it," he suggests. "Give them something to really talk about."

"Don't you dare," I warn, though there's no heat behind it.

He winks. "Your secret's safe with me, Dr. Winters. For now."

* * *

Noah

I walk into the paramedic station two days after our HR disclosure and immediately sense the shift in atmosphere. The usual morning banter dies down as I enter, replaced by sidelong glances and poorly concealed whispers. My locker suddenly becomes the most interesting thing I've ever seen as I focus on organizing my gear.

"Morning, Supervisor Love Doctor," Jackson calls out from across the room, drawing scattered laughter.

I manage a tight smile. "Morning, Jackson."

Dani slides up beside me, her voice low. "Ignore him. He's just jealous because his Tinder profile hasn't had a match in three months."

"I heard that!" Jackson protests.

"You were meant to," Dani fires back, then turns to me. "How are you holding up?"

I shrug, checking my supplies. "It's fine. Expected, I guess."

But it isn't fine. The constant attention makes my skin itch. I didn't anticipate becoming the hospital's favorite soap opera overnight.

Captain Rivera emerges from her office, clipboard in hand. "Alright, assignments for today. Bennet and Ramirez, you're in rig three."

Dani gives me a supportive nudge as we head toward our ambulance. I catch Captain Rivera watching me with an expression I can't quite read before she turns away.

During vehicle check, Marcus from the night shift approaches. "Hey,

Noah, congrats man. Dr. Winters seems like a good guy."

His sincerity catches me off guard. "Thanks, Marcus. He is."

"My wife was his patient last year when she had that bad reaction. Said he was the best doctor she'd ever had." He pauses. "Just wanted you to know not everyone around here is being weird about it."

I feel a knot in my chest loosen slightly. "I appreciate that."

Our first call is straightforward—elderly woman with chest pain that turns out to be indigestion. As we're completing paperwork at Metropolitan General, I spot Dr. Chen at the nurses' station. She gives me a friendly nod, which feels like a small victory.

"You know," Dani says as we head back to the rig, "I think people are mostly just surprised. Dr. Winters has this reputation for being all work, no play."

"He's not what people think," I reply, unable to keep the warmth from my voice.

"Obviously. The man practically melts when you're in the room."

The radio crackles to life—motor vehicle accident with multiple injuries. We respond code three, lights and sirens.

At the scene, we find two cars with significant damage. I slip into work mode, assessing and triaging. The driver of the first vehicle has a possible head injury and needs immediate transport.

"Ramirez, you take the passenger from car two. I've got this one," I direct, already establishing an IV line.

We arrive at Metropolitan General with our patients, and I'm met by Dr. Kapoor rather than Liam. Part of me is relieved—we're still figuring out how to navigate our professional interactions under scrutiny.

As I'm giving report, I notice two nurses whispering and looking in my direction. Dr. Kapoor catches it too.

"Some people need to focus more on medicine and less on gossip," she says loudly enough for them to hear. They quickly disperse, looking embarrassed.

After we transfer care, Dr. Kapoor stops me. "Noah, a moment?"

My stomach tightens. "Yes, doctor?"

"I've known Liam for years. He's an exceptional physician and a good friend." She pauses, studying me. "I've never seen him like this before."

I'm not sure how to respond. "Like what?"

"Happy," she says simply. "Distracted, but happy. Just thought you should know."

The unexpected endorsement leaves me speechless. I manage a nod before rejoining Dani.

Back at the station during lunch, I'm grabbing coffee when Captain Rivera approaches.

"Bennet, got a minute?"

I follow her to her office, bracing myself. She closes the door and sits behind her desk.

"I need to address something," she begins. "There's been some chatter about your relationship with Dr. Winters."

"I understand, Captain. We've completed all the necessary HR—"

She holds up a hand. "I'm aware. That's not my concern. What matters to me is whether this affects your work."

"It won't," I say firmly.

"Good. Because some of the crew have expressed... concerns."

My jaw tightens. "What kind of concerns?"

"Questions about favoritism, mostly. Whether you'll get special treatment at the hospital, or if Dr. Winters will prioritize your patients."

The suggestion makes my blood boil. "Liam would never compromise patient care. And neither would I."

She studies me for a moment. "I believe you. But perception matters in our line of work. You'll need to be above reproach."

"I understand."

"Just so you know" she adds, her expression softening slightly, "I told them to mind their own business and focus on their own damn jobs."

The afternoon brings a steady stream of calls. During a drop-off at Metropolitan, I catch Liam in the hallway, deep in conversation with a resident. He looks up, sees me, and his entire face brightens before he carefully composes himself, offering a professional nod.

I return the gesture, fighting my own smile.

Later, as Dani and I restock supplies, Jackson and his partner Torres join us.

"So, Bennet," Torres starts, "you gonna put in a good word for us with the boss's boyfriend?"

Before I can respond, Jackson cuts in. "Lay off, man."

Torres looks surprised. "What? I'm just saying he's got an in now."

"And I'm saying he doesn't need one," Jackson retorts. "Noah was a damn good medic before Dr. Winters, and he's a damn good supervisor now."

The unexpected defense leaves me momentarily stunned.

Torres raises his hands in surrender. "No offense meant."

"None taken," I say, though that's not entirely true.

As they walk away, I turn to Jackson. "Thanks for that."

He shrugs. "Just facts. Besides, anyone who's seen you two work a trauma together knows there's something special there. Medical soulmates or whatever."

His words stay with me through the rest of the shift. For every sideways glance or whispered comment, there's been someone like Marcus, Dr. Kapoor, or even Jackson balancing the scales.

When my phone buzzes with a text from Liam asking about dinner, I realize something important: the opinions that truly matter are already in my corner.

* * *

I stand outside the conference room, straightening my uniform tie for the third time. The brass nameplate on the door reads "Ethics Committee" in stern, official lettering. My palms are sweaty despite the hospital's aggressive air conditioning.

"You've got this," I mutter to myself, checking my watch. Two minutes until my scheduled appearance.

I've replayed the incident with Mrs. Grimes countless times in my head. I know I followed protocol. I know I did right by my patient. But sitting before a panel of hospital administrators ready to judge my actions feels like being called to the principal's office—if the principal could end your career.

The door opens, and Dr. Kapoor appears. Despite being Liam's friend, her expression is purely professional.

"Mr. Bennet, we're ready for you now."

I follow her into the room where five people sit at a long table. I recognize Dr. Hadley at the center, flanked by the hospital's legal counsel, the head of nursing, and two other physicians I've seen but never worked with directly.

"Please take a seat," Dr. Hadley gestures to a solitary chair facing the panel.

I sit, folding my hands on the table to keep them from fidgeting.

"This is an informal hearing regarding the complaint filed by Eleanor Grimes concerning your conduct on April 15th," Dr. Hadley begins. "We've reviewed the written statements, but we'd like to hear your account of the events directly."

I take a deep breath. "Thank you for the opportunity to address this matter. On April 15th, my partner and I responded to a call at 247 Oakwood Drive for a female patient reporting chest pain."

I describe our arrival at Mrs. Grimes' home, how we found her sitting upright in her living room, alert and oriented but distressed.

"Her initial vitals showed elevated blood pressure and tachycardia. She complained of substernal chest pain radiating to her left arm, which had begun approximately forty minutes before she called 911."

Dr. Kapoor nods, making notes. "And this is when the alleged delay occurred?"

"No, doctor. We immediately administered aspirin and placed her on oxygen while preparing for transport. The delay Mrs. Grimes references in her complaint occurred when she insisted on changing clothes before going to the hospital."

The head of nursing leans forward. "She wanted to change clothes during a potential cardiac event?"

"Yes. She was wearing a nightgown and robe and refused to leave until she could put on 'proper clothes.' I explained that time was critical and that we needed to transport immediately, but she was adamant."

"Did you physically prevent her from changing?" Dr. Hadley asks.

"No, sir. I would never physically force a competent patient. I did, however, make it very clear that any delay could impact her outcome, especially if she was having a heart attack. I also explained that the hospital would provide a gown and that her dignity would be maintained."

"And how did she respond?" asks one of the physicians I don't know.

"She accused me of being disrespectful and insisted I wait outside while she changed. My partner and I stepped into the hallway but left the door open. I continued to urge her to reconsider, explaining that minutes matter in cardiac cases."

"How long was the delay?" Dr. Kapoor asks.

"Approximately seven minutes from when she first insisted on changing to when we finally got her on the stretcher. Our documentation shows we were on scene for a total of fifteen minutes, which is within protocol for a cardiac call with a cooperative patient."

The legal counsel, who has been silent until now, speaks up. "Mrs. Grimes alleges that you spoke to her in a condescending manner and that you 'manhandled' her onto the stretcher."

I shake my head firmly. "I was direct about the medical risks of delaying care, which may have come across as stern, but I was never disrespectful. As for 'manhandling,' we assisted her onto the stretcher using standard transfer techniques. She was unsteady due to her condition, and we needed to ensure she didn't fall."

"The ER notes indicate she was diagnosed with acute coronary syndrome," Dr. Hadley says. "Did you convey the seriousness of her condition?"

"Absolutely. I told her directly that her symptoms were consistent with a heart attack and that immediate treatment was essential to prevent permanent heart damage or worse."

I detail the rest of the transport, including our pre-hospital interventions and smooth handoff to the emergency department.

"Looking back," Dr. Kapoor asks, "is there anything you would have done differently?"

I consider this carefully. "I might have explained more clearly why changing clothes could wait—perhaps emphasizing that the hospital staff regularly handle these situations with dignity. But regarding the urgency of transport and my insistence that we leave immediately? No, I stand by that decision. In cardiac cases, tissue death begins within minutes. Every delay increases risk."

The panel members exchange glances, and Dr. Hadley nods slightly.

"Do you have anything else to add, Mr. Bennet?"

"Only that I understand Mrs. Grimes was frightened, and sometimes fear manifests as resistance or anger. I don't take her complaint personally. My only concern was—and remains—her medical outcome."

Dr. Kapoor closes her folder. "Thank you for your candid responses, Mr. Bennet. We appreciate your time and your detailed account of the incident."

"Is there any additional information you need from me? Patient care logs, my partner's corroboration, anything at all?"

"Not at this time," Dr. Hadley responds. "We'll review everything presented today along with the medical records and other statements we've gathered."

Dr. Kapoor stands, signaling the end of the hearing. "We'll be in touch with the results of our investigation and any determinations regarding disciplinary action, if deemed necessary. You're free to return to your duties."

I rise from my chair, thanking the committee for their time. As I turn to leave, I feel a curious mix of relief and lingering tension. The hardest part is over, but the waiting begins.

* * *

I balance two pizza boxes and a six-pack of beer as I fumble with my keys outside my apartment door. After a twelve-hour shift, I'd normally collapse on the couch, but knowing Liam's coming over gives me a second wind.

Inside, I find Marcus's door closed with a note taped to it: "At Jen's again. Text before you bring company over next time."

I roll my eyes. It's the third time this week he's cleared out when Liam visits. I appreciate the privacy, but the passive-aggressive notes are getting old.

I set everything down on the kitchen counter and fire off a quick text to Liam: *Just got home. Food's here when you are.*

While waiting, I change into a comfortable t-shirt and jeans, then straighten up the living room. Not that Liam cares—he's seen my place at its worst—but I still make the effort.

My phone pings with his reply: *Pulling up now. Brought wine to class up your beer selection.*

I laugh and head downstairs to meet him. When the elevator doors open, he steps out looking exhausted but smiling. His hair is slightly disheveled, and his shirt is wrinkled from a long day, but he's still the best thing I've seen all day.

"Hey," I say, taking the wine bottle from him and leaning in for a quick kiss.

"Hey yourself." He follows me up the stairs. "Please tell me that's pepperoni I smell."

"Pepperoni and mushroom for me, that weird pineapple abomination you like for you."

"Hawaiian is a classic," he protests as we enter my apartment. "Your taste is just unrefined."

"Says the man who eats fruit on pizza."

We settle on the couch with our respective pizzas and drinks. Liam kicks off his shoes and props his feet on my coffee table, looking around.

"Marcus out again?" he asks between bites.

I nod. "Left another note. He's getting annoyed about having to clear out whenever you're over."

"I noticed the collection of passive-aggressive Post-its on your fridge." Liam takes a sip of wine. "That's the third time this week, isn't it?"

"Fourth if you count Saturday morning." I grab another slice. "He's being dramatic."

We eat in comfortable silence for a moment before Liam sets down his pizza and turns to face me.

"You know, this arrangement isn't really fair to Marcus," he says thoughtfully. "Or to us, for that matter."

"What do you mean?"

"Well, we're basically splitting our time between two places, neither of which is really ours. You're displacing your roommate, and my place is too small for two people to comfortably exist together."

My heart rate picks up. "What are you suggesting?"

Liam looks directly at me, his expression serious but warm. "Maybe we should consider moving in together. Sooner rather than later."

I nearly choke on my beer. "You want us to move in together?"

"Is that crazy?" His confidence wavers slightly. "I mean, we practically live together already, just with the inconvenience of two locations and a grumpy roommate."

I set my beer down, processing his words. We've only been dating for a few weeks, but he's right—we spend almost every night together. And there's that inexplicable connection we've had from the start.

"It's not crazy," I say slowly. "It's just... sudden."

"Too sudden?" There's vulnerability in his question.

I reach for his hand. "No. Not too sudden. Actually, I'd love that."

The smile that breaks across his face makes my chest tighten. "Really?"

"Really." I squeeze his hand. "But where? Your place is too small, and this place has Marcus."

"We could find a new place. Something that's ours from the start." He shifts closer to me on the couch. "Somewhere closer to the hospital, maybe?"

The idea of creating a home with Liam—a space that belongs to both of us—fills me with unexpected joy.

"I'd need to give Marcus notice," I say, already mentally planning. "And we'd need to figure out timing with our leases."

"Details," Liam waves dismissively, then grows serious again. "Are you sure about this? I know it's fast."

I look at him—this man who somehow knew exactly what I needed before I did from the moment we met—and any doubt evaporates.

"I'm sure. It feels right." I pull him closer. "Besides, think of all the money we'll save on rent."

He laughs. "Very romantic."

"I'm practical like that." I lean in to kiss him, tasting wine and that ridiculous pineapple pizza. "But seriously, I want this. I want us to have our own place."

Liam's eyes soften. "Then let's do it. Let's find a place that's ours."

The pizza sits forgotten as we start discussing neighborhoods and must-haves for our new place. Liam wants a decent kitchen; I argue for proximity to good coffee. We both agree on needing enough space for visitors and a short commute to the hospital.

It should feel terrifying—this massive step forward—but instead, it feels like the most natural progression in the world.

I look at Liam across the couch, his hair falling slightly over his forehead as he scrolls through apartment listings on his phone. We've spent the last hour discussing neighborhoods, commute times, and whether we need one bathroom or two. The reality of what we're planning suddenly hits me— we're actually going to do this. We're going to live together.

Something important occurs to me.

"You know," I say, setting my beer down on the coffee table, "there's one thing we haven't tested for compatibility yet."

Liam looks up from his phone, eyebrow raised. "What's that?"

I clear my throat, suddenly feeling a flutter of nervousness. "Well, if we're going to live together, we should probably make sure we're compatible in... all areas."

"All areas?" His expression is puzzled for a moment before understanding dawns. "Oh."

"Yeah." I shift on the couch to face him more directly. "We've done almost everything else, but not that. And I wouldn't want to sign a lease only to find out we're not... you know, physically compatible in that way."

A smile plays at the corner of his mouth. "Are you propositioning me, Noah Bennet?"

"I'm being practical," I counter, though I can't help smiling too. "Very practical. It's an important compatibility test."

Liam sets his phone down and moves closer to me on the couch. "And here I thought I was being too forward suggesting we move in together."

"Well, one of us has to be the bold one." I reach out and take his hand, suddenly serious. "But only if you want to. No pressure."

His eyes meet mine, and I see the same mixture of desire and nervousness I'm feeling. We've been taking things slow in that department—plenty of making out and sleeping in the same bed, but always stopping short of going all the way. At first, it was about not rushing, then it became this unspoken thing between us, a line we hadn't crossed yet.

"I want to," he says softly. "I've wanted to for a while now."

My heart races. "Me too."

"So why haven't we?"

I shrug, trying to articulate something I've been feeling but haven't put into words. "Maybe because everything else has been so intense between us from the start. The way we connect at work, how we always seem to know what the other is thinking... I think part of me was afraid this would be too much. Too intense."

Liam nods slowly. "I know what you mean. It's like we've been savoring each step."

"Exactly." I squeeze his hand. "But if we're going to live together..."

"Then we should know if we're compatible in bed," he finishes, a hint of mischief in his eyes.

"For practical reasons," I add with mock seriousness.

"Of course. Very practical." He leans in closer. "What if we're terrible together?"

I laugh. "Somehow I doubt that."

"Confident, are we?"

"Let's just say I have a good feeling about this." I reach up to brush my thumb across his cheek. "Like everything else between us, I think we'll just... know what to do."

His expression softens, and he leans into my touch. "Noah?"

"Yeah?"

"Take me to bed."

The directness of his request sends a jolt through me. I stand up, pulling him with me, and lead him toward my bedroom. At the doorway, I pause and turn to face him.

"You're sure?" I ask, needing to hear it one more time.

In answer, Liam steps forward and kisses me, slow and deliberate. When he pulls back, his eyes are dark with want. "I'm sure. I want this. I want you."

Those words break something loose in me—a restraint I've been holding onto without even realizing it. I pull him into my room, closing the door behind us even though we have the apartment to ourselves.

We stand at the foot of my bed, suddenly shy despite everything we've already shared. It's different this time—we both know where this is leading.

"So," Liam says with a nervous laugh, "how do we...?"

"Maybe we just start like we usually do," I suggest, "and see where it goes?"

He nods, and I step closer, resting my hands on his waist. The familiar gesture helps ease the tension, and when I kiss him, it feels like coming home. His hands find their way to my shoulders, then my neck, then tangle in my hair as the kiss deepens.

We've done this part dozens of times, but tonight there's a new urgency, a knowledge that we're not going to stop. I walk him backward until his legs hit the bed, and we tumble onto it together, laughing as we bounce on the mattress.

"Smooth," Liam teases, his hands already working at the hem of my t-shirt.

"I have my moments." I lift my arms to help him remove my shirt, then return the favor with his.

The sight of him half-dressed in my bed makes my breath catch. We've seen each other shirtless before, but the context makes everything different, more charged.

"You're beautiful," I whisper, running my hand along his side.

He blushes slightly. "So are you."

There's a moment of hesitation as we look at each other, both aware of the threshold we're about to cross.

"Noah?" Liam's voice is soft.

"Yeah?"

"I love you."

It's not the first time he's said it, but in this moment, it carries a different weight. I lean down to kiss him, pouring everything I feel into it.

"I love you too," I murmur against his lips. "Now, let's see how compatible we really are."

I lower myself onto Liam, our bare chests pressing together as we kiss. The weight of his confession—"I love you"—still hangs in the air between us, making every touch more significant. His skin is warm against mine, and I can feel his heartbeat racing to match my own.

"I've thought about this," I whisper against his neck, trailing kisses down to his collarbone. "More than I should admit."

Liam's fingers trace patterns on my back, sending shivers along my spine. "Me too. Especially during those long shifts when I'd catch glimpses of you in the ER."

I smile against his skin. "So unprofessional, Dr. Winters."

"Completely." His hands slide down to my waist, fingers hooking into my belt loops. "You're a terrible distraction."

Our eyes meet, and that familiar connection flares between us—the same inexplicable understanding that lets us work in perfect sync during traumas. Only now, it's channeled into something entirely different, something intimate and private.

I reach between us to unbutton his jeans, my fingers brushing against his stomach. His breath hitches, and I pause, savoring his reaction. When I pull down his zipper, he lifts his hips to help me slide the denim down his legs.

"Your turn," he murmurs, his hands already working at my jeans.

We undress each other slowly, each new expanse of skin an exploration. When we're down to our underwear, I hover above him, taking in the sight of him nearly naked in my bed. His chest rises and falls with quick breaths, and I can see the outline of his arousal pressing against the fabric of his boxer briefs.

"You're staring," he says, a hint of vulnerability in his voice.

"Can't help it." I trace my finger along the waistband of his underwear. "You're gorgeous."

A flush spreads across his chest and up his neck. I lean down to kiss him again, deeper this time, as my hand slips beneath the elastic. He gasps into my mouth when my fingers wrap around him, his hips bucking upward.

"Noah," he breathes, the sound of my name on his lips sending heat through my body.

I stroke him slowly, watching his face as pleasure overtakes him. His eyes flutter closed, lips parting, completely unguarded in a way I've never seen him at the hospital. This is Liam without his professional armor, without the careful control he maintains around others.

His hands aren't idle, exploring my body with the same precision he uses in medical procedures. When he pushes my underwear down and takes me in his hand, I nearly lose my composure.

"Wait," I manage to say, stilling his movement. "I want—I need—"

"What do you need?" His eyes are dark, focused entirely on me.

"I need to feel you. All of you." I kiss him again, trying to convey what I can't quite articulate. "I have... things. In the nightstand."

Liam reaches over to open the drawer, finding the condoms and lube I keep there. He hands them to me, his expression a mixture of desire and trust that makes my chest tight.

"Are you sure?" I ask one more time.

He pulls me down for a kiss. "I've never been more sure of anything."

I slowly peel away the last scraps of fabric separating us until we're skin against skin in all our glorious nakedness. Then I take my sweet time exploring every inch of Liam's body with my fingers and lips—kissing him deeply as I work my hand down his chest to tease at his nipples until they stiffen under my touch. His body arches into me with a gasp as I lower myself between his legs.

I take him fully into my mouth, savoring the salty-sweet taste of him on my tongue as I work him slowly with lips and teeth. He moans low in his throat when I take him deep into my throat without warning. His hands tangle in my hair, holding me close as he rocks his hips against my face. When I finally pull back to meet his gaze with swollen lips and heavy-lidded eyes, he's flushed from head to toe.

"Please," he breathes urgently. "I need you inside me."

I reach for the lube with trembling fingers as Liam spreads his legs wider in invitation. I slick up both myself and him with teasing strokes until he's panting hard beneath me. Then I line up carefully and push inside him inch by slow inch. Liam cries out sharply at the sudden intrusion before melting into a soft groan of pleasure once I bottom out deep inside.

The heat of him gripping me tight is almost overwhelming—like coming home after years away only to find it even better than memory served. For a moment we're frozen together, both just breathing raggedly through the intense sensation of being joined so intimately. The connection between us feels electric—every nerve ending alight with sensation that goes far beyond physical touch alone.

Finally I have to move or go mad from want. I pull back slow until just the tip remains inside before sliding forward again with agonizing slowness. Liam bucks underneath me each time with little sounds spilling unbidden from his kiss-swollen lips—a symphony of need that inflames my blood like wildfire. Each thrust builds on the last until we're moving together fast enough for sweat to slide slick between our straining bodies locked tight around mine in the relentless rhythm of sex.

All too soon Liam finds his peak sobbing my name like an incantation while spurting hot release over his chest in erratic pulses that milk me through my own shuddering climax. We collapse together after boneless in a tangle of damp limbs and sheets as our breathing slows from frantic to merely unsteady.

I roll us onto our sides still intimately joined so I can look into Liam's passion-hazed eyes with tender intensity as I cup his flushed cheek.

"Well," Liam finally says, pushing back against me making me moan in pleasure as I sink deeper into him still, "I think we can confirm we're compatible in all areas."

I laugh. "Very compatible. We should probably test it again, though. For science."

"Oh, how soon do you think that can happen?" Liam asks innocently, wiggling his butt teasing me even more.

Liam stops and look seriously back at me, his hair disheveled and his eyes soft. "I love you, Noah. Not just because of... this." He gestures between us. "But because of everything. The way you know what I'm thinking. The way you make me laugh. The way you care about your patients."

I lean down for a gentle kiss. "I love you too. And I can't wait to find a place with you. Our place."

He settles back against my chest, and I feel his smile against my skin. "Our place," he repeats softly. "I like the sound of that...."

"Not to change the subject but I'm ready to go now, so get on your stomach and stick your rear in the air for me" I say enthusiastically.

Liam's eyes darken with desire at my command. He rolls over slowly, giving me a tantalizing view of his lean body as he settles onto his stomach. Then, with deliberate slowness, he lifts his hips and spreads his legs, presenting himself to me like an offering.

I drink in the sight of him, splayed out before me so wantonly. My gaze traces every curve of his back, down to where it narrows at the waist, and then flares out again into the perfect globes of his ass. I can see how wet he is already, glistening between those enticing cheeks.

"You want this?" I ask hoarsely, giving myself a few slow strokes to regain control. "You want me to take you from behind?"

"Yes," Liam breathes into the mattress. "Please."

I kneel behind him and run my hands over the smooth skin of his buttocks reverently. I spread them apart and lean in close to press hot openmouthed kisses along that forbidden crevice. He shudders beneath me as I delve deeper with each kiss until I'm teasing at his hole with my tongue.

"Noah," he mumbles incoherently against the pillow when I slip my tongue inside him for a quick taste.

"Get ready," I warn him breathlessly as I reach for more lube. My fingers find him slick and swollen from earlier but still tight around their invasion. He pushes back eagerly into each stroke until he's moaning loudly and bucking wildly against my hand.

"I need you," Liam begs shamelessly between harsh pants. "Need you now."

With one last swirl of my fingers inside him I withdraw reluctantly only to push back in again thicker than before - stretching that ring of muscle wide around the blunt head of my cock until it slips past to bury itself deep in one smooth thrust all the way to the hilt.

"Oh fuck!" Liam cries out sharply clenching down hard around me once before relaxing enough for me to begin sliding slowly out just far enough that only the tip remains before pushing back in just as slowly - relishing each delicious drag along sensitive nerves until our rhythm picks up pace.

The obscene slap of skin on skin echoes through the room mingled with panting breaths and low groans spilling unbidden from both our mouths as we move faster together locked tight around mine driving home over and over until finally Liam bucks underneath me finding release spurting hot pearly ropes of come across them. As he releases, his hole milks my cock pushing me over the edge and I slam into him filling his hole with spurt after spurt of come.

We collapse boneless to the bed, lying in the sticky mess of come. We're both panting heavily, riding out the orgasm together still.

"I think it's safe to say we're not going to have a boring bedroom life" Liam says, between breaths.

I grin lazily at Liam, savoring the pleasant feeling of release spreading through my body. "Not boring is an understatement." I lean down to kiss him softly. "I think we've found yet another area where we're perfectly in sync."

Liam hums contentedly against my lips. His body feels perfect beneath me, our bodies still joined intimately. Neither of us seems eager to separate.

Eventually, we untangle ourselves, the need for food overpowering our desire to remain wrapped in each other's arms. I pull on a pair of sweatpants while Liam borrows my robe, too large on his frame but endearing in how it envelops him.

In the kitchen, I reheat the pasta we'd abandoned earlier, while Liam opens a bottle of wine. The domesticity of it feels natural, as though we've been doing this dance for years instead of months.

"Hungry?" I ask, sliding a plate in front of him at the small kitchen table.

"Starving," he admits, the candlelight I've impulsively lit catching the gold flecks in his eyes. "Apparently certain activities work up quite an appetite."

I pour wine into his glass, settling across from him. "I've been thinking," I say, watching him twirl pasta around his fork.

"Dangerous," Liam teases.

"That thing that happens between us." My voice grows more serious. "That connection. Have you ever experienced anything like it with anyone else?"

Liam's fork pauses halfway to his mouth. "Never. Not even close." He sets the fork down, giving the conversation his full attention. "I've been wondering about it since that first trauma case together."

"Like I'd known you forever?" I lean forward, elbows on the table. "Yeah. It was... disorienting. I kept thinking I must have met you before."

"But we hadn't."

"No." I take a sip of wine, gathering my thoughts. "I've never experienced anything like it with anyone else. The way we just... know what the other is thinking. What the other needs."

Liam's finger traces the rim of his wine glass. "My grandmother would have called it soul recognition."

"Soul recognition?"

"She believed some souls know each other across lifetimes. That when they meet again, there's an instant recognition."

I consider this, surprised at how the concept resonates. "Like we've done this before? Been together before?"

"Maybe." Liam looks slightly vulnerable sharing something so fanciful. "Or maybe it's something more scientific. Some kind of neurological synchronicity."

"The paramedic in me wants a rational explanation," I admit. "But honestly? Nothing about what happens between us feels rational."

"Dr. Chen once joked that we share a brain."

I laugh, reaching for his hand across the table. "If we're getting metaphysical about it, I prefer the soul theory. I like thinking that maybe I've been finding my way to you for longer than just this lifetime."

Liam's expression softens, and I watch emotions play across his face. "It should scare me—how easy this is, how natural. But it doesn't."

"What does it feel like to you?" I ask, my thumb drawing circles on his palm.

"Like coming home," he says without hesitation. "Like all my life, I've been trying to solve a puzzle with missing pieces, and then you walked in and suddenly the picture was complete."

I feel my eyes glisten in the candlelight. "Maybe we'll never know why. Maybe it's spiritual. Maybe it's scientific. Maybe it's just extraordinary luck."

"Does it matter?" Liam asks.

I shake my head, smiling. "No. The why doesn't change anything. It doesn't change how I feel when I'm with you."

Liam stands, pulling me to my feet and into his arms. "Then let's stop questioning it and just be grateful we found each other."

"In this lifetime," I add with a playful smile.

"In this lifetime," Liam agrees, pressing his forehead to mine. "And hopefully the next."

Chapter 11

Liam

Isquint at my phone's screen, trying not to smile too obviously in the middle of the ED. Noah's latest text shows a sun-drenched living room with high ceilings and windows that stretch nearly floor to ceiling.

Imagine waking up to that light every morning. Plus, big enough for activities... ;)

My cheeks warm as I type back: *What activities did you have in mind?*

Three dots appear immediately. *I'm thinking a sex swing would fit perfectly in that corner. Great stress relief after long shifts.*

I nearly choke on my coffee, glancing around to make sure no one's reading over my shoulder. *I'll add it to my Amazon cart right now. Prime delivery by tomorrow.*

That's why I love you. Always efficient.

Those three words still send a flutter through my chest, even after hearing them every day for weeks. It's been a month since we decided to move in together, and we've spent every night at my place, tangled in each other's arms. Now we're finally getting serious about finding our own space.

I click through the listing photos. The kitchen is sleek with granite countertops, and there are two bathrooms—a definite upgrade from my cramped apartment.

Rent's a bit high, I text, *but look at that kitchen. I promise not to burn it down. I'll protect you from evil kitchen appliances. That's what boyfriends are for.*

A trauma alert blares over the intercom, and I pocket my phone with a sigh. Back to reality.

"What do we have?" I ask, entering Trauma One where nurses are already preparing equipment.

"MVA, two patients incoming. First is male, 40s, possible internal bleeding and head trauma," Chen says, snapping on gloves.

I wash my hands quickly and gown up. "ETA?"

"Three minutes. Paramedics on scene reported unresponsive initially, now Glasgow 12."

Not Noah's unit, then. I push away the irrational disappointment. We see each other every night, yet I still find myself hoping he'll roll through those ambulance bay doors during my shifts.

The trauma goes smoothly—stabilization, CT scan, then up to surgery for a small bleed. I'm updating charts at the nurses' station when my phone buzzes again.

It's another listing from Noah. This one has hardwood floors throughout and a balcony.

Imagine morning coffee out there, his text reads. *Or evening wine. Or midnight...*

Midnight what? I reply, already knowing where his mind is going.

Stargazing, Dr. Winters. What were YOU thinking?

I laugh out loud, earning a curious glance from Mira.

"House hunting?" she asks, peering over my shoulder.

"Noah keeps sending listings. We're hoping to find something next month when both our leases are up."

She grins. "The hospital pool on you two moving in together paid out last week. Now they're betting on engagement timelines."

"We've only been together two months!" I protest, but the thought sends a warm current through me. It should feel too fast, too soon, but nothing with Noah follows normal timelines. From that first day in the trauma bay, we've operated on our own schedule.

"When you know, you know," Mira shrugs. "You two are disgustingly perfect together."

My phone buzzes again. Another listing, this one closer to the hospital.

Seven-minute drive to work, Noah texts. *More sleep before shifts.*

More time for other things too, I reply.

Exactly what I was thinking. Great minds.

I check the patient board—two in rooms waiting for test results, but nothing urgent. I take the moment to call the number on the listing.

"Hello, I'm interested in viewing the apartment on Maple Street? Tomorrow afternoon would be perfect."

After arranging the viewing, I text Noah the details. His response is immediate: *I'll be there. Can't wait to see our future home.*

Our future home. The phrase settles in my chest, solid and right.

The afternoon passes in a blur of patients—abdominal pain, broken wrist, chest pain that turns out to be anxiety. Between cases, Noah and I exchange more listings, each message filled with plans and possibilities.

This one has a huge shower, he texts with a listing that's slightly above our budget.

Water conservation is important, I reply. *Showering together is just being environmentally conscious.*

You're so noble. Always thinking of the planet.

During a rare quiet moment, I find myself staring at the listings we've saved, imagining Noah's books mixed with mine on shelves, his clothes hanging next to mine, our shoes jumbled together by the door. It's been just a month of spending every night together, but I can no longer picture my life any other way.

My phone buzzes with an incoming call from Noah.

"Hey," I answer, stepping into the empty doctors' lounge. "Everything okay?"

"Just finished a call near your place. Found the perfect housewarming gift for wherever we end up."

"Let me guess—a sex swing?"

His laugh travels through the phone, warm and familiar. "Close. It's a bookstore with a clearance sale. Medical texts half off. Thought you might want to add to your light bedtime reading collection."

"You know me too well."

"That's the idea, isn't it?" His voice softens. "I'm heading back to the station, but I'll see you tonight?"

"Your toothbrush is waiting patiently in my bathroom."

"Along with half my wardrobe at this point."

"Just practicing for the real thing."

After we hang up, I find myself smiling at nothing in particular. A month ago, I worried that living together might be rushing things. Now, I can't imagine waiting any longer.

* * *

Noah

I'm halfway through my paperwork when my phone buzzes. Sliding it from my pocket, I see Dr. Kapoor's name on the screen. My stomach tightens as I answer.

"Noah Bennet."

"Noah, it's Dr. Kapoor. I wanted to call you personally with the news." His voice carries a warmth that immediately loosens the knot in my chest. "The Ethics Committee has completed their review of Mrs. Grimes' complaint."

I straighten in my chair, my pen forgotten on the half-completed incident report. "And?"

"You've been fully cleared of any wrongdoing. The committee found that you followed all protocols appropriately and maintained professional conduct throughout the incident."

The tension I've been carrying for weeks releases in a rush. "Thank you. That's... that's great news."

"The committee noted that your documentation was exceptionally thorough, which helped establish the timeline and validate your account. Mrs. Grimes' claims about your conduct were determined to be unfounded."

I lean back, eyes closed, letting the relief wash over me. "I appreciate you calling me directly."

"Of course. You're an exemplary paramedic supervisor, Noah. No one who knows your work doubted the outcome." There's a pause before he adds, "A formal letter will be placed in your file, but I thought you'd want to know immediately."

"You have no idea how much. Thanks again, Dr. Kapoor."

After ending the call, I sit motionless for a moment, processing the news. The complaint has been hanging over me for weeks, a constant weight even when I tried to ignore it. Now it's gone.

I pick up my phone again and text Liam.

Cleared of the complaint. Official letter coming soon.

His response comes almost immediately.

Never doubted it for a second. Dinner tonight to celebrate?

I smile at the screen.

Absolutely. My place at 7?

I'll bring champagne. So proud of you.

The rest of my shift passes in a blur. I handle a minor fender bender, a fall at a nursing home, and an asthma attack at an elementary school. Through it all, I feel lighter than I have in weeks.

When I return to the station, Captain Rivera calls me into her office.

"Just got word from the hospital," she says, leaning against her desk. "Congratulations, Bennet."

"Thank you, Captain."

"For what it's worth, I knew Grimes was full of it from the start. You're one of my best." She crosses her arms. "But this is a good reminder for all supervisors. Documentation matters."

"Lesson definitely learned."

"Good." She nods toward the door. "Now go finish your shift. I think your crew has something planned."

Sure enough, when I walk into the break room, there's a small cake with "NOT GUILTY" written in blue icing. Dani, Marcus, and the rest of the crew break into applause.

"You guys didn't have to do this," I say, genuinely touched.

"Are you kidding?" Dani cuts into the cake. "This is as much for us as it is for you. Do you know how insufferable you've been since this complaint?"

"I have not been—"

"You've been checking your phone every five minutes and sighing like a teenager." She hands me a slice. "Plus, we were worried if things went south, we'd have to deal with Dr. Winters in a bad mood. That man is scary when he's upset."

I laugh, accepting the cake. "He's not scary."

"To you, maybe. The rest of us mere mortals find him intimidating as hell when he's in doctor mode."

Marcus raises his coffee cup. "To Noah, who can now stop looking like someone kicked his puppy every time his phone rings."

"Very funny." I take a bite of cake. It's grocery store vanilla, but right now it tastes better than any five-star dessert.

By the time I get home, shower, and change, it's nearly seven. I've just finished straightening up when there's a knock at the door.

Liam stands in the hallway, champagne in one hand and a small gift bag in the other. His smile lights up his entire face.

"Congratulations, Noah." He steps inside, setting the champagne on the counter before wrapping his arms around me.

I pull him close, burying my face in his neck and breathing in the clean scent of his cologne. "Thanks. It feels good to have it officially over."

"I told you there was nothing to worry about." He pulls back, eyes meeting mine. "You're the most professional paramedic I've ever worked with."

"Even when I'm undressing you with my eyes during trauma calls?"

He laughs, the sound warming me from the inside. "Especially then. Multitasking is a valuable skill in emergency medicine."

I take the champagne and search for glasses while Liam places the gift bag on the counter.

"What's this?" I ask, nodding toward the bag.

"Just a little something to mark the occasion."

Inside, I find a small silver keychain in the shape of an ambulance. When I turn it over, there's an engraving: *For the man who always knows the right call. -L*

"This is perfect." I run my thumb over the engraving. "Thank you."

"I had it made last week. I was that confident in the outcome."

I pour champagne into two glasses and hand one to Liam. "To unwavering faith in my professional judgment."

"And to moving forward." He clinks his glass against mine. "No more looking over our shoulders."

We settle on the couch, Liam tucked against my side. The warmth of him, solid and real, grounds me in the moment.

"You know what this means?" I ask, tracing patterns on his arm with my fingertips.

"What?"

"We can focus completely on apartment hunting now. No more distractions."

He groans dramatically. "Is that really what you want to talk about tonight?"

"No." I set our glasses on the coffee table and turn to face him. "But I thought I should mention it before I get too distracted by other things."

"Other things?" His eyes darken as he leans closer.

"Very important things."

As my lips find his, I feel the last of the tension melt away. Whatever comes next—new apartment, new challenges—we'll face it together, without this shadow hanging over us.

* * *

Liam

I'm finishing up the chart for Mrs. Peterson's gallstones when Mira appears at my shoulder.

"Dr. Hadley's looking for you," she says. "Someone from Boston General is here to see you. They're in the small conference room."

"Boston General?" I frown, setting down my tablet. "Did they say what it's about?"

"No, but they look important. Nice suit, fancy briefcase."

I mentally run through my recent research publications, wondering if one of them caught someone's attention. "Thanks, Mira. Can you keep an eye on bed four? His abdominal CT results should be back soon."

The small conference room is tucked away from the bustle of the emergency department. I knock before entering, finding a woman in her fifties with silver-streaked hair and a tailored navy suit.

"Dr. Winters," she says, rising to shake my hand. "I'm Dr. Eleanor Vaughn, Director of Physician Recruitment for Boston General Hospital. Thank you for making time to see me."

"Of course," I reply, taking the seat across from her. "Though I'm a bit surprised. I wasn't expecting visitors from Boston."

She smiles, opening a leather portfolio. "I'll get right to it. We've been following your work in emergency medicine, particularly your research on trauma protocols and your clinical outcomes. Boston General is establishing a new Emergency Medicine Innovation Fellowship, and we'd like to offer you the inaugural position."

My heart rate kicks up. Boston General is one of the top teaching hospitals on the continent. "I'm... honored. What exactly would this fellowship entail?"

"It's a two-year position with the possibility of permanent placement afterward. You'd split your time between clinical work in our Level I trauma center and developing new protocols based on your research. The fellowship comes with dedicated research funding, teaching opportunities with Harvard Medical, and mentorship from Dr. William Chen."

"Dr. Chen?" I lean forward. "The William Chen who pioneered the RAP-ID trauma assessment protocol?"

"The very same. He specifically requested you after reading your paper on anticipatory trauma team coordination."

I sit back, momentarily speechless. William Chen is a legend in emergency medicine. The opportunity to work with him is something most emergency physicians would kill for.

Dr. Vaughn slides a folder across the table. "This contains the formal offer, including salary details, benefits, and research funding allocation. The fellowship would begin in three months, giving you time to transition your responsibilities here."

I open the folder, and the numbers make me blink. The salary is nearly double what I make at Metropolitan General, plus research funding that would allow me to pursue projects I've only dreamed about.

"This is... extremely generous," I manage.

"We believe in investing in exceptional talent, Dr. Winters. Your work shows remarkable innovation, and frankly, your clinical outcomes speak for themselves." She pauses. "There is, however, a time consideration. We need your decision within two weeks. If you decline, we'll need to offer the position to our second choice candidate."

Two weeks. My mind races through the implications. Boston is over a thousand miles away. Away from Metropolitan General. Away from Noah.

Noah.

"I understand," I say, trying to keep my voice steady. "This is a significant opportunity that requires careful consideration."

"Of course." Dr. Vaughn hands me her business card. "Please call me with any questions. We'd be delighted to fly you out to Boston to tour the facilities and meet with Dr. Chen before you make your final decision."

We shake hands, and I escort her out of the conference room, my mind already spinning with possibilities and complications. As I return to the emergency department, the folder feels heavy in my hands.

Mira raises an eyebrow when she sees my expression. "Good news or bad news?"

"I'm... not sure yet." I tuck the folder into my locker. "Boston General is offering me a fellowship."

Her eyes widen. "Boston? As in Massachusetts?"

"The very same."

"That's... wow. Are you going to take it?"

I lean against the wall, suddenly needing the support. "I don't know. It's an incredible opportunity. Working with William Chen, research funding, Harvard teaching appointment..."

"But?" Mira prompts, knowing me too well.

"But it's in Boston." The implications hang in the air between us. Noah and I are just finding our rhythm, planning our future together. We're about to move in together, for god's sake.

"Have you told Noah yet?"

"Just found out myself." I check my watch. "He's on shift until eight. We're supposed to meet at my place after."

Mira squeezes my arm. "This is big, Liam. Whatever you decide, make sure it's what you really want."

The rest of my shift passes in a blur. I treat patients on autopilot while my mind keeps returning to the folder in my locker. By the time I clock out, I've mentally rehearsed a dozen different ways to tell Noah about the offer.

As I drive home, I can't stop thinking about what this fellowship would mean for my career. Working with William Chen could open doors I never imagined possible. The research funding alone would allow me to develop protocols that could save countless lives.

But then there's Noah. Noah, who understands me in ways no one else ever has. Noah, who I'm falling in love with more deeply each day. Noah, who I can't imagine being separated from by half a continent.

I pull into my parking space, turn off the engine, and sit in silence, the weight of the decision pressing down on me. Two weeks to choose between the career opportunity of a lifetime and the man who might be the love of my life.

* * *

Liam

The key to my apartment turns easily, but I pause before pushing the door open. The folder from Dr. Vaughn sits heavy in my bag, its contents potentially explosive to the life Noah and I are building. I take a deep breath and enter.

Noah's already made himself at home, his shoes by the door, music playing softly from the kitchen. The smell of garlic and herbs fills the apartment.

"Hey," I call out, dropping my keys in the bowl by the door.

Noah appears in the kitchen doorway, dish towel slung over his shoulder, smile lighting up his face. "Perfect timing. Pasta's almost ready."

I cross to him, drawn like a magnet. His arms wrap around me, solid and warm, and for a moment I forget everything else. His lips find mine, tasting faintly of the red wine I spot open on the counter.

"Rough day?" he asks against my mouth.

"Just... complicated." I pull back slightly. "You didn't have to cook."

"Wanted to. You've been working doubles all week." He kisses me again, then returns to the stove. "Go change. Food in five."

In the bedroom, I change out of my work clothes, carefully placing Dr. Vaughn's folder in my desk drawer beneath some papers. Out of sight, but definitely not out of mind.

When I return to the kitchen, Noah's plating pasta with a simple tomato sauce, fresh basil scattered on top. He hands me a glass of wine.

"To finding our perfect apartment tomorrow," he toasts, clinking his glass against mine.

Right. Our apartment viewing. The one we scheduled weeks ago for the place on Maple Street with the built-in bookshelves Noah thought would be perfect for my medical texts.

"To tomorrow," I echo, the words sticking in my throat.

Over dinner, Noah tells me about his shift—an elderly man who fell at home but was more concerned about missing his favorite TV show than his broken hip, a teenager who got her hand stuck in a vending machine, the usual emergency medicine chaos we both thrive in.

"You're quiet tonight," he observes as we finish eating. "Something on your mind?"

This is it. The perfect opening.

"I—" I start, then falter. "Just tired. It was back-to-back traumas today."

Noah nods, accepting my lie without question. He trusts me completely. The guilt twists in my stomach.

"Leave the dishes," he says, standing and taking my hand. "I've got a better idea for how to help you relax."

In the bedroom, Noah's hands are gentle but insistent, stripping away my clothes and my defenses. His mouth traces patterns across my skin that make me forget everything but the sensation of his touch. I lose myself in him, in us, in the connection that still feels miraculous every time.

"I love how you respond to me," he murmurs against my collarbone. "Like you know what I'm going to do before I do it."

I pull him closer, desperate to silence the voice in my head that keeps whispering *Boston* with every beat of my heart. Noah's body covers mine, familiar now but still thrilling. I arch into him, seeking more contact, more distraction.

"Liam," he breathes, his eyes finding mine in the dim light. "You're with me, right? You seem somewhere else."

"I'm here," I promise, pulling him down for a kiss. "Just thinking how lucky I am to have found you."

His expression softens. "That's funny. I was thinking the same thing."

We move together, finding that perfect rhythm that comes so naturally to us. I try to memorize everything—the weight of him above me, the catch in his breath when I touch him just right, the way his eyes never leave mine. As if some part of me already knows these moments are precious, possibly numbered.

After, when we're tangled in the sheets, Noah's head resting on my chest, I gather my courage.

"Noah, there's something I need to tell you."

He props himself up on one elbow, face serious. "That sounds ominous."

"It's not... well, it's complicated." I take a deep breath. "Today, I had a meeting with—"

My phone chirps with a message. Noah reaches for it on the nightstand, glancing at the screen.

"It's from Dr. Chen," he says, handing it to me. "911 trauma alert, all hands. Multiple GSWs coming in from a shooting downtown."

I sit up, reading the message. "Five critical patients, ETA ten minutes."

Noah's already pulling on his clothes. "I'll drive you. Marcus texted earlier—they're calling in off-duty medics too."

And just like that, the moment's gone. We dress quickly, moving around each other with practiced efficiency. As Noah grabs his keys, I hesitate by the desk drawer containing Dr. Vaughn's folder.

"Liam? You coming?"

I turn away from the drawer. "Right behind you."

In the car, Noah drives with focused intensity while I mentally prepare for the chaos awaiting us at the hospital. The fellowship offer retreats to the back of my mind, temporarily overshadowed by the immediate crisis.

"What were you going to tell me?" Noah asks as we near the hospital, red and blue lights from ambulances already visible in the distance.

I look at his profile, strong and determined in the dashboard light. How do I tell him that I've been offered my dream job, but it would mean leaving him behind? How do I choose between the career I've worked toward my entire life and the man who makes that life worth living?

"It can wait," I say finally. "Let's focus on saving lives first."

Noah nods, accepting my delay without question. The trust in that simple gesture makes my chest ache.

As we pull up to the ambulance bay, already crowded with vehicles and medical personnel, I know I've only postponed the inevitable. Soon, I'll have to tell him. Soon, I'll have to decide.

But not tonight.

Act 3

Chapter 12

Noah

I slam the car into park outside the ambulance bay, barely registering that I've straddled two spaces. Liam's already got his door open before we've fully stopped.

"I'll see you in there," he says, his voice shifting into that clinical tone I've come to recognize—the one that separates the man I love from the doctor he becomes when lives are at stake.

We sprint through the automatic doors, separating immediately. Liam heads for the trauma rooms while I make for the staff locker room to grab scrubs. The call had been vague—multiple GSWs, critical condition, all hands needed. Standard emergency protocol, but something about tonight feels different. A heaviness in the air I can't explain.

Three minutes later, I'm rushing toward Trauma One, tying my scrub pants as I go. The corridor buzzes with controlled chaos—nurses rushing IV fluids, techs prepping equipment, Dr. Chen barking orders as she passes.

I push through the doors and freeze.

The patient on the table is young—early twenties, dark hair matted with blood and dirt. His body is torn open across the abdomen, with another wound visible on his upper thigh. But it's not the wounds that stop me cold.

It's the flannel shirt cut open across his chest. Red and black checkered. The motorcycle boots still on his feet, and the vivid red road rash that covers most of his body.

"Motor vehicle accident," someone says. "Truck hit him going 100 kilometres an hour and knocked him right off his bike on the highway."

My lungs seize. The room tilts.

"Noah!" Liam's voice cuts through the fog. He's gowned up, hands already bloody as he works with Dr. Hayes to control the bleeding. "I need you here. Now."

I move forward automatically, my body functioning while my mind fractures. The patient's face comes into view—not my brother's, of course not my brother's—but young like Matt was. Riding his bike, just like Matt did. Wearing the same damn flannel pattern Matt always wore.

"BP's crashing," a nurse calls out.

"We need more units," Liam orders. "Noah, pressure here."

I place my hands where he indicates, feeling warm blood pulse between my fingers. The sensation is horrifically familiar.

"He was wearing his biking gear," I hear myself say. "Why is he all torn up like this if he was wearing it?"

Dr. Hayes glances up. "He was going too fast for it to do much. If he hadn't had it on, he wouldn't even be alive on this table."

Just like Matt. Exactly like Matt.

"Noah, focus," Liam says sharply, his eyes finding mine across the table. There's recognition there—he knows something's wrong but can't stop to ask. "I need you here with me."

"I'm here," I manage, but my voice sounds distant to my own ears.

The trauma bay becomes a blur of activity. Blood transfusions. Chest tubes. Ultrasound showing massive internal bleeding. The metallic smell of blood mixed with antiseptic burns my nostrils.

"He's in V-fib!" someone shouts.

The paddles come out. The body arches. Falls back. No conversion.

"Again!"

Another shock. Nothing.

I'm performing compressions now, feeling ribs crack beneath my hands. Pushing. Counting. Sweating. The room spins around me as memories collide with present reality.

Matt on a similar table. Matt's blood on similar floors. Matt's life slipping away while I stood helpless in a waiting room, not yet a paramedic, not yet able to help.

"Time of death, 21:47," Dr. Hayes says finally, stepping back from the table.

My hands are still on the patient's chest. Still pushing. Someone—Liam—gently pulls them away.

"Noah. He's gone."

I look up, meeting Liam's eyes. The room has emptied somewhat, the immediate crisis ended in the worst possible way. Only Liam, a nurse documenting, and Dr. Hayes remain with me and our patient. Our dead patient.

"His name was Tyler," the nurse says quietly, reading from the wallet they've retrieved. "Tyler Malone. Nineteen years old."

The same age Matt was.

"I need some air," I mutter, stripping off my gloves and gown.

I stumble out of the trauma room, down the hall, through a service door, and into the night air behind the hospital. My legs give out and I slide down the wall until I'm sitting on the concrete, head between my knees, gasping for breath that won't come.

The door opens a minute later. Liam crouches beside me, still in his trauma gown, blood smeared across the front.

"Noah. Talk to me."

I can't look at him. "Matt died the same way."

Understanding dawns on his face. He sits beside me, shoulder pressed against mine.

"Motor cycle accident, he got knocked off and shredded to bits on the asphalt. He was only nineteen." My voice breaks. "They couldn't save him either."

Liam doesn't speak, just wraps an arm around my shoulders and pulls me against him. I realize I'm shaking.

"I became a paramedic so I could save people like him. Like Matt. And I couldn't do anything. Just like before."

"We all did everything possible," Liam says softly. "Sometimes everything isn't enough."

"I know that. Logically, I know that." I wipe at my face, surprised to find it wet. "But tonight, it was like watching Matt die all over again."

Liam presses his forehead against my temple. "I'm so sorry."

We sit in silence for several minutes, the cool night air gradually slowing my racing heart. Hospital sounds filter through the walls—pages over intercoms, distant voices, the hum of machinery keeping other patients alive.

"I should have told you about Matt sooner," I say finally. "About exactly how he died."

"You told me what you could when you were ready," Liam says. His hand finds mine, fingers intertwining. "There's no timeline for sharing grief."

I turn to look at him, this man who somehow understands me without explanation. "I need to call his family. Tyler's family. I know what they're about to go through."

Liam nods. "We'll do it together."

Chapter 13

Liam

The fellowship folder sits in my desk drawer like a ticking bomb. It's been five days since Dr. Vaughn handed me the opportunity of a lifetime, and I still haven't told Noah. Every night, I promise myself I'll bring it up, and every night, I find a reason not to.

Tonight, I stand in my kitchen watching Noah chop vegetables for stir-fry, his movements precise and confident. He's wearing one of my t-shirts that's slightly too small for him, stretching across his shoulders as he works. The domesticity of it all makes my chest ache.

"You're staring again," Noah says without looking up from the cutting board. "Something on your mind?"

My heart hammers against my ribs. This is it. This is the moment I should tell him.

"Just thinking about how good you look in my clothes," I say instead, the coward's way out.

Noah smiles, that crooked half-grin that still makes my stomach flip. "You should see what I look like out of them."

"I believe I'm familiar with that view."

He laughs and tosses a piece of bell pepper at me. I catch it and pop it in my mouth, trying to ignore the guilt settling heavy in my gut.

"How was your shift?" I ask, changing the subject.

"Pretty standard. Mrs. Lowell's back again—ankle's still giving her trouble." Noah scrapes the vegetables into the wok with a satisfying sizzle. "Oh, and I looked at that apartment on Maple Street during my lunch break."

My stomach drops. "You did?"

"Yeah, it's perfect, Liam. Two bedrooms, that study nook you wanted, walking distance to the hospital." His eyes shine with excitement. "The lease is up in exactly a month, which lines up perfectly with ours ending. I put in an application."

"You put in an application?" The words come out sharper than I intend.

Noah's hands pause over the wok. "I thought... we talked about this. You said you liked that one best from the listings."

"I know, I just..." I run a hand through my hair. "You should have waited for me to see it."

"I texted you about it this afternoon."

I pull out my phone and see three unread messages from Noah, complete with photos of the apartment. I'd been in meetings all day, including one with Dr. Hadley about quarterly performance reviews, and hadn't checked my phone.

"I'm sorry," I say, feeling like an even bigger jerk. "I didn't see these."

Noah studies my face. "What's going on with you lately? You've been distracted all week."

This is it. This is the moment I need to tell him. I take a deep breath. "I—"

My pager goes off with perfect, terrible timing. I check it—trauma alert.

"You've got to be kidding me," I mutter.

Noah's already turning off the stove. "Go. We'll talk later."

"Noah—"

"It's fine." He kisses me quickly. "Go save lives, Dr. Winters. I'll put this in the fridge for when you get back."

I grab my keys and rush out, both relieved and frustrated by the interruption.

* * *

Liam

I dash into the ER, already tying my trauma gown as I push through the double doors. The page was for a rollover MVA with multiple victims, but when I arrive, Dr. Chen is already handling the first patient.

"Winters, good timing," she says. "We've got three more coming in. I need you on the second ambulance."

I nod, grateful for the distraction from my personal chaos. For the next two hours, I lose myself in the familiar rhythm of trauma medicine—assess, stabilize, treat. It's the one place where everything makes sense, where I know exactly what to do and say.

By the time we've stabilized all four victims, my shoulders ache with tension. I'm peeling off my gloves when Dr. Hadley's voice comes over the intercom.

"Attention all staff. Brief meeting in the main nurses' station in five minutes."

I groan internally. The last thing I need is another administrative update when I should be figuring out how to tell Noah about Boston.

The nursing station fills quickly with the day shift staff. I spot Mira leaning against the far wall and slide next to her.

"Any idea what this is about?" I ask.

She shrugs. "Probably another lecture about charting or insurance codes."

Dr. Hadley clears his throat, commanding the room's attention. "Thank you all for gathering on such short notice. I wanted to personally introduce a temporary addition to our surgical team."

I'm barely listening, mentally rehearsing what I'll say to Noah tonight. Maybe I should just lay it all out—the fellowship, the opportunity, the timeline. Ask him what he thinks about long distance.

"...pleased to welcome Dr. Jason Mercer from Ottawa General, who will be joining us for the next three weeks as part of our surgical exchange program."

My head snaps up so fast I nearly give myself whiplash.

Jason. My Jason. Ex-Jason.

And there he is, stepping up beside Dr. Hadley with that same confident smile that once charmed me completely. He looks exactly the same—tall, dark-haired, with those intense blue eyes and perfect teeth. The sight of him hits me like a physical blow.

"Thank you, Dr. Hadley. I'm excited to observe Metropolitan General's innovative approach to emergency medicine and cardiothoracic cases," Jason says, his voice carrying that slight Quebecois lilt I once found endearing. "I look forward to working with all of you."

His eyes scan the crowd and lock with mine. His smile widens.

I can't breathe.

"Liam," Mira whispers beside me. "Isn't that—"

"Yes," I manage, my voice strangled.

"The cheating ex?"

"Yes."

"Holy shit."

Dr. Hadley continues with administrative announcements, but I hear nothing. My hands tremble as I pull out my phone and text Noah.

911. Jason is here. At the hospital. As a visiting surgeon.

Noah's response is immediate.

Your ex Jason??

Yes. Please come. I can't do this.

On my way. 10 minutes.

The meeting breaks up, and I try to slip away, but Jason's voice calls out behind me.

"Liam! Wait up!"

I consider pretending I didn't hear him, but we're in a crowded room. People are already watching, curious about the new doctor calling my name. I force myself to turn around.

"Jason," I say, my voice carefully neutral. "What a surprise."

He grins and pulls me into an unwanted hug. I stand stiffly, arms at my sides.

"Look at you! Emergency department director now, I hear. Always knew you'd do well." He claps my shoulder like we're old friends. "Why didn't you tell me you were at Metropolitan? I would have called ahead."

"That would have required having my number, which I specifically didn't give you after—" I stop myself, aware of the audience. "It's been a long time."

"Water under the bridge, right?" Jason laughs easily. "We were young. People make mistakes."

The casual dismissal of how he destroyed me makes my blood boil. Before I can respond, I feel a presence at my side and smell the familiar scent of Noah's aftershave.

"Hey babe," Noah says, his hand possessively finding the small of my back. "Got here as fast as I could."

Relief floods through me. Noah's here. I'm not facing this alone.

Jason's eyes narrow slightly as he takes in Noah, clearly assessing the situation.

"Jason, this is Noah Bennet," I say, finding my voice. "Noah, this is Dr. Jason Mercer."

"Ah, more than just Noah Bennet, I think," Jason says with a knowing smile. "You must be the new boyfriend. I'm the ex-lover. Ottawa days."

Noah's hand tightens slightly on my back, but his face remains pleasant. "Paramedic supervisor. Nice to meet you." His tone suggests it's anything but nice.

"Paramedic? Interesting choice, Liam." Jason's smile doesn't reach his eyes. "Always thought you'd end up with another surgeon."

"I prefer someone with integrity," I reply, finding courage in Noah's presence.

Jason laughs like I've made a joke. "We should grab dinner while I'm here. Catch up properly. I have so many stories about Liam's residency days."

"We're pretty busy," Noah interjects smoothly, stepping slightly between us. "Moving in together next month, lots of packing to do."

The territorial move isn't subtle, but I'm grateful for it. Jason's eyebrows raise.

"Moving in already? That was fast. How long have you two been together? Two months?"

"Three," Noah corrects. "When you know, you know."

Jason looks like he wants to say more, but a nurse approaches me with a chart.

"Dr. Winters, your patient in bed four needs discharge orders."

"I'll be right there," I tell her, never more grateful for an interruption.

"Duty calls," Noah says to Jason. "Nice meeting you."

Noah's hand guides me away, a physical barrier between me and my past. As we walk toward bed four, he whispers, "You okay?"

"No," I admit. "But I'm better now that you're here."

I walk with Noah toward the nurse's station, my mind racing faster than my heart. Jason's sudden appearance has thrown me completely off balance. Three years of carefully constructed distance shattered in an instant.

"Let's step outside," I whisper to Noah once I've signed the discharge papers. "I need air."

Noah nods, his hand still protectively at my back as we slip out the ambulance bay doors. The late afternoon sun casts long shadows across the parking lot, and I inhale deeply, trying to clear my head.

"So that's Jason," Noah says, leaning against the wall. His voice is casual, but I can see tension in his shoulders. "He's exactly what I pictured."

"What, an arrogant ass?"

Noah's laugh is short, strained. "That too. But I meant successful. Polished. A cardiothoracic surgeon who looks like he stepped out of a medical drama."

I turn to face him, surprised by the undercurrent in his voice. "Noah?"

He runs a hand through his hair, not meeting my eyes. "Is this going to be a problem? Him being here?"

"For me? No. I'm over him."

"That's not what I meant." Noah shifts his weight, uncomfortably. "Is it going to be a problem for us?"

The vulnerability in his question catches me off guard. I reach for his hand. "Why would it be?"

"Come on, Liam." Noah's fingers tighten around mine. "A surgeon and a paramedic standing side by side? It's pretty clear which one fits better in your world."

I stare at him, shocked. "That's what you're worried about? Professional status?"

"I saw how he looked at me when you introduced us. Like I was some curiosity. 'A paramedic? Interesting choice, Liam,'" Noah mimics Jason's condescending tone perfectly. "And he's not wrong, is he? You're technically dating someone below your class, career-wise."

"Below my—" I sputter, anger flaring. "Is that really what you think? That I see you as beneath me?"

Noah sighs, his shoulders slumping. "No. Not you. But everyone else does. The hospital hierarchy is real, Liam. Doctors at the top, then nurses, then the rest of us. I've lived with those dynamics my entire career."

"That's not how I see things."

"Maybe not. But having your ex show up—a successful surgeon who probably makes three times what I do—it just highlights the gap, you know?" Noah's voice drops. "Makes me wonder if you're settling."

The raw insecurity in his confession knocks the wind from me. This confident man who strides into trauma rooms without hesitation, who faces death daily with steady hands, is standing before me afraid he's not good enough.

"Noah, look at me." I step closer, framing his face with my hands. "I left Jason because he cheated, yes. But even before that, I was miserable. Our relationship was all about appearances, about being the power couple everyone envied. It was hollow."

Noah's eyes search mine. "And us?"

"Us?" I smile, stroking my thumb across his cheek. "With you, I can breathe. When we're together, whether we're saving lives or just making dinner, everything clicks into place. You understand parts of me I've never shared with anyone."

"But—"

"No buts. You're not some consolation prize, Noah. You're the prize I never thought I'd find." I press my forehead against his. "Jason being here changes nothing. If anything, seeing him just reminds me how lucky I am to have found you instead."

Noah's arms circle my waist, pulling me closer. "I'm sorry. I don't usually let insecurities get to me like this."

"Don't apologize. We're both figuring this out." I kiss him softly. "Besides, you should have seen Jason's face when you called me 'babe' and mentioned moving in together. That territorial move was hot as fuck."

Noah laughs, some of the tension leaving his body. "That wasn't entirely for show. When I saw him touch you, something primal kicked in."

"I noticed." I lean into him, grateful for his solid presence. "For the record, I love that you're a paramedic. The way you connect with patients, how you stay calm in chaos—that's who you are, not just what you do."

"And what about the money?" Noah asks, his tone lighter but still carrying a hint of concern. "Surgeons make a lot more than paramedic supervisors."

"I have enough money. What I need is you." I pull back to meet his eyes. "The way we work together, the way we understand each other—that's worth more than any salary."

Noah's smile reaches his eyes this time, but I can still see lingering doubt there. "You're sure? Having him around won't bring up old feelings?"

"The only feelings Jason brings up are regret that I wasted so many years with him and relief that it ended before I was in too deep." I kiss Noah again, more firmly. "You're who I want. No competition."

Noah nods, his arms tightening around me. "Okay. I believe you."

My pager beeps, interrupting the moment. I check it with a sigh. "Back to the ER. You heading out?"

"Yeah, shift starts in thirty." Noah releases me reluctantly. "Will I see you tonight?"

"Count on it. Your place or mine?"

"Mine. Marcus is visiting his parents."

I smile. "Perfect. I'll bring takeout."

As we part ways at the ambulance bay, Noah kisses me one more time. His smile is almost back to normal, but I can see the shadow of doubt still lingering in his eyes.

Chapter 14

Liam

I stare at the chart in my hands, reading the same line for the third time without absorbing a single word. The name glares back at me: Robert Winters, 67, admitted with chest pain and shortness of breath.

My father.

The father I haven't spoken to in eight years.

"Dr. Winters?" Nurse Kelly's voice cuts through my haze. "The patient in Trauma 3 is asking for you specifically."

"I know." My voice sounds distant, even to my own ears. "I'll be there in a minute."

I duck into the bathroom, splashing cold water on my face. The mirror reflects a version of myself I barely recognize – pale, wide-eyed, jaw clenched tight enough to crack teeth. I take three deep breaths, the way I taught myself in medical school during panic attacks before exams.

This is just another patient. Another case. I can do this.

The walk to Trauma 3 feels like traversing a minefield. Each step brings me closer to a past I've spent years trying to outrun. I pause outside the door, squaring my shoulders before pushing it open.

Robert Winters looks smaller than I remember. His once-robust frame appears diminished against the white hospital sheets. The monitor shows elevated blood pressure, tachycardia. His eyes – the same blue as mine – lock onto me the moment I enter.

"Liam." His voice is raspy, weaker than I recall. "You came."

I focus on the chart, avoiding his gaze. "Mr. Winters, I'm Dr. Winters. I understand you're experiencing chest pain?"

"Eight years and that's how you greet your old man?" He attempts a laugh that dissolves into a cough.

I reach for my stethoscope. "I need to listen to your heart."

"Ironic, isn't it?" He smiles weakly. "My heart's what brought me here. To you."

I press the stethoscope to his chest, listening for abnormalities while mentally reciting cardiac assessment protocols. Anything to maintain professional distance. "Deep breath, please."

He complies, then says, "Your mother would be proud, seeing you in that white coat."

The mention of Mom sends a jolt through me. I move the stethoscope, keeping my expression neutral. "Any history of cardiac issues?"

"Started taking medication for hypertension about five years ago." He pauses. "You'd know that if you returned my calls."

I make a note on the chart. "Any other medical conditions I should know about?"

"Liam, please. Can we talk like father and son for just a minute?"

"I'm your doctor right now." I step back, creating physical distance to match the emotional gulf between us. "I need to order an ECG and some blood work."

"I've changed, Liam." His hand reaches for mine, but I shift away. "After your mother died, I was lost. The drinking, the anger... I know I hurt you."

I write orders for troponin levels and a full cardiac panel. "A technician will be in shortly for your ECG."

"I'm sober now. Four years." His voice cracks. "I've been trying to find you, to make amends."

The words hit like a physical blow. Four years of sobriety. Four years of attempts to contact me that I've systematically ignored or blocked.

"Congratulations," I say, the word coming out colder than intended. "I'll send someone in to draw blood."

"Your number changed. I tried the hospital, but they wouldn't give me your information." He shifts, wincing slightly. "I didn't plan on having chest pain to finally see you, but I guess the universe works in strange ways."

I check his oxygen levels, focusing on the numbers rather than the man. "Your O2 sat is good. Pain level now?"

"About a six." He sighs. "It was worse earlier. Felt like an elephant on my chest."

I nod, making another note. "We'll get you something for the pain after we rule out cardiac issues."

"I'm proud of you, seeing you here. You always wanted to help people. Even as a little kid." His eyes grow misty. "Remember when you set up that 'hospital' for neighborhood pets? You were maybe seven?"

Despite myself, the memory surfaces – a card table in our garage, bandages made from torn sheets, "medicine" concocted from juice and water. Mom had helped me make a white coat from an old shirt.

"Mr. Winters, I need to check on your test results." I move toward the door.

"Liam, wait." His voice holds a desperation that stops me. "I know I don't deserve your forgiveness. What I did... how I treated you and your mother... I can't take it back."

I stand frozen, hand on the door.

"But I'm dying, son."

I turn slowly. "What?"

"Not today, probably." He attempts a smile that doesn't reach his eyes. "Stage four pancreatic cancer. Diagnosed three months ago."

The clinical part of my brain immediately calculates survival statistics – dismal at best. The son part... I'm not ready to acknowledge what that part feels.

"That's why finding you became so urgent." He takes a shaky breath. "The chest pain is probably nothing. Just stress and the cancer. But when they asked which hospital to take me to, I said Metropolitan General. Because of you."

I'm suddenly aware of the weight of my stethoscope around my neck, the pressure of my pager against my hip. The symbols of the profession I chose to help people, to heal them.

But some wounds run too deep for medicine.

"I'll order an oncology consult," I say finally, my voice barely audible. "They'll want to review your treatment plan."

"Liam—"

"I need to check your results." I push through the door, escaping into the hallway where I lean against the wall, breathing hard.

Eight years of silence. Eight years of building a life without him in it. And now this.

My pager beeps – lab results ready. I push off the wall, straightening my coat.

I have a job to do. A father to treat. And somehow, I need to find a way to be both doctor and son in a situation where I'm not sure how to be either.

***

Noah

I'm halfway through my shift when my phone buzzes with a text from Liam.

My father's in Room 4. Don't know what to do.

My stomach drops. I know Robert Winters was admitted yesterday, but Liam hasn't said much about it since then. The terse message tells me everything I need to know about his state of mind.

"Dani, I need to swing by Metro General for fifteen," I tell my partner as we finish restocking our rig.

She gives me a knowing look. "Liam emergency?"

"Family stuff. Cover for me with Rivera?"

"Go. But you owe me coffee for a week."

I find Liam in the doctors' lounge, hunched over a tablet displaying what must be his father's chart. His shoulders are rigid, face drawn into tight lines I've never seen before. This isn't my confident, composed Liam. This is someone drowning.

"Hey," I say softly, closing the door behind me.

He doesn't look up. "His pancreatic enzymes are elevated. Cancer's spreading faster than projected. Pain management is becoming an issue."

I sit beside him, not touching yet, giving him space. "How are you holding up?"

"Fine." The word comes out brittle. "Just reviewing treatment options."

"Liam."

He finally meets my eyes, and the raw pain I see there knocks the breath from my lungs. I reach for his hand, and he lets me take it, his fingers cold against mine.

"I don't know what to do," he whispers. "He's asking for me. Not as his doctor—as his son."

"And you don't want to see him?"

"I don't know what I want." Liam sets the tablet down with precise movements. "Part of me wants to walk into that room and tell him exactly what he did to us. Another part wants to pretend he doesn't exist. And then there's this other voice saying I should forgive him because he's dying, and isn't that what good people do?"

I squeeze his hand. "There's no rulebook for this."

"You'd forgive him," Liam says, not as an accusation but as if stating a fact.

"You don't know that."

"I do. You have that... goodness in you. You're basically the equivalent of a human golden retriever."

I shake my head. "This isn't about what I would do. Tell me about him. You've never really talked about your parents."

Liam's quiet for so long I think he might not answer. Then he pulls his hand from mine and stands, pacing the small confines of the lounge.

"My father was a functional alcoholic for most of my childhood. Respected economics professor by day, mean drunk by night." His voice takes on a clinical detachment that breaks my heart. "He never hit us—that's what my mother always emphasized when I got older. 'At least he never hit us.' As if that was the bar."

"What did he do?" I ask gently.

"He'd come home and find fault with everything. The house wasn't clean enough. Dinner wasn't right. I was too quiet or too loud or too... something." Liam stops pacing, staring at nothing. "He'd berate my mother until she cried, then he'd lock himself in his study with a bottle. Some nights he'd throw things. Break dishes. Punch walls."

I stay silent, letting him continue at his own pace.

"When I was fourteen, my mother finally left him. We moved across town, and for the first time, I remember her smiling without that tension in her eyes." Liam's voice softens. "She went back to nursing school. Started rebuilding her life. Then when I was in college, she was diagnosed with breast cancer."

"I'm sorry," I murmur.

"She fought it for three years. My father showed up at the hospital once—once—during that entire time. He was drunk. Created a scene. Security had to remove him." Liam's hands clench into fists. "She died during my second year of medical school. At her funeral, he tried to act like the grieving husband. I told him to leave and never contact me again."

"And he respected that until now?"

"He sent cards for a while. I returned them unopened. Eventually, he stopped." Liam turns to me, his expression haunted. "Now he shows up with terminal cancer, claiming sobriety, wanting... what? Absolution? A relationship? It's too late for either."

I stand and approach him slowly. "What do you want, Liam?"

"I want him not to be my problem." His voice cracks. "Is that terrible? My father is dying down the hall, and I'm angry he's forcing me to deal with him again."

"It's not terrible. It's human."

"He says he's changed. Four years sober. But you know what alcoholics are like—masters of manipulation."

I take his hands in mine. "You don't have to decide right now. You don't owe him anything."

"But what if—" Liam swallows hard. "What if I regret not giving him a chance? When he's gone?"

The question hangs between us, impossible to answer. I pull him into my arms, and he comes willingly, burying his face against my shoulder. I feel the shudder that runs through him, the way he fights against breaking down completely.

"I'm here," I whisper into his hair. "Whatever you decide, I'm with you."

"I don't know what to do," he repeats, voice muffled against my uniform.

"Then we figure it out together. One step at a time."

He pulls back slightly, eyes red-rimmed but dry. "You have patients. A shift."

"Dani's covering. I'm where I need to be."

Liam takes a shaky breath. "I think... I think I need to talk to him. Not forgive him. Not yet. But listen, at least."

"Want me to come with you?"

He considers this, then shakes his head. "No. This first conversation needs to be just us. But knowing you're here helps."

I brush my thumb across his cheek. "I'll wait. As long as it takes."

* * *

Liam

I stand outside my father's hospital room, my hand frozen on the door handle. Noah's supportive presence behind me gives me strength, but this is a conversation I need to have alone.

"I'll be right here," Noah says, squeezing my shoulder.

I nod, pushing the door open before I can change my mind.

Robert Winters looks smaller in the hospital bed than I remember him. His once-imposing frame now gaunt, his face yellow with jaundice. The monitors beep steadily, marking time between us.

"Liam." His voice cracks. "You came back."

"I'm still your doctor," I say, keeping my voice clinical as I pick up his chart. "Nothing more."

"I understand." He shifts in the bed, wincing with pain. "But I'm grateful you're here at all."

I scan his latest test results, noticing something immediately. His ACTH levels are significantly elevated, which could be exacerbating his symptoms and pain levels.

"Your hormone levels are off," I say, focusing on the medical rather than the emotional. "It might be making your condition worse."

"Is that fixable?" A flicker of hope crosses his face.

"Manageable," I correct, writing a new prescription. "I'm changing your medication. It should help with the pain and some of the other symptoms."

He nods, watching me work. The silence between us grows heavy with unspoken words.

"Liam, I know I have no right to ask for forgiveness—"

"You're right." I cut him off, finally looking directly at him. "You don't."

His eyes drop to his hands.

"Do you have any idea what you did to us?" The words escape before I can stop them, my professional veneer cracking. "To Mom? To me?"

"I was sick, Liam. The drinking—"

"Was a choice. Every bottle was a choice. Every time you chose alcohol over your family was a choice."

"You're right." He doesn't argue, which somehow makes it worse. "I can't change the past."

"No, you can't." I set down his chart harder than necessary. "You can't erase the nights Mom cried herself to sleep. You can't take back the birthdays you missed or the parent-teacher conferences you were too drunk to attend."

He absorbs each accusation like a physical blow.

"And you know what the worst part was?" My voice drops. "When Mom got sick, when she needed someone, you weren't there. I had to watch her die alone because you couldn't be bothered to be a father or a husband when it actually mattered."

"I know." Tears stream down his weathered face. "I know, and I'll regret it until my dying day."

"Which is coming sooner rather than later," I say coldly, immediately regretting the cruelty but unable to take it back.

He nods, accepting this too.

I take a deep breath, steadying myself. "I can never forgive you for what you did to our family over the years."

"I understand."

"But I'm going to help you." I pick up his chart again. "Because that's who I am. That's who Mom raised me to be, no thanks to you."

I write down another note. "I'm referring you to Dr. Melissa Kang. She's the leading oncologist at this hospital, specializing in pancreatic cancer. I'll use my staff discount to get you priority treatment."

His eyes widen. "Liam, I can't ask you to—"

"You're not asking. I'm doing it." I finish writing and look at him again. "I won't be part of your life. I won't be the son you suddenly want now that you're facing your mortality. But I'll be the better man and take care of you medically, even though you never took care of us when we needed you."

The room falls silent except for the steady beeping of monitors.

"Your mother would be proud of the man you've become," he finally says.

"Don't." I hold up my hand. "Don't talk about her. You lost that right a long time ago."

He nods, tears still tracking down his face.

I continue reviewing his chart, making notes about his treatment plan. "The new medication should start working within 24-48 hours. Dr. Kang will be in to see you tomorrow morning. She'll discuss your options for palliative care and possibly some experimental treatments that might extend your timeline."

"Thank you," he whispers.

I finally look at him, really look at him—this broken shell of the man who once terrified me. I feel nothing but a hollow ache where anger used to burn.

"I'm not doing this for you," I say quietly. "I'm doing it because it's the right thing to do. Because I refuse to be the kind of person who abandons others when they need help the most."

The unspoken comparison hangs between us.

"I'll check on you tomorrow," I say, closing his chart. "Professionally."

As I reach the door, his voice stops me.

"Liam? That young man waiting for you outside... he seems like a good person."

I pause, hand on the doorknob. "He is. The best I've ever known."

"Then you've found something I never did," my father says softly. "Someone who loves you for who you are. Don't take that for granted."

I don't respond, but as I step out of the room, the weight on my chest feels slightly lighter. Not gone—perhaps it never will be—but lighter.

Noah stands immediately, concern written across his face. "How did it go?"

I take his hand, needing his warmth. "I told him I'd help him medically, but that's it. I can't be the son he suddenly wants now."

Noah pulls me into his arms, and I let myself be held, finding strength in his embrace.

"You did the right thing," he murmurs against my hair. "The kind thing."

"Did I?" I ask, my voice muffled against his shoulder.

"You're helping him even though he hurt you. That takes incredible strength." Noah pulls back to look at me. "It's one of the reasons I love you."

I lean my forehead against his, drawing comfort from his presence. "Let's go home."

Chapter 15

Noah

I straighten my tie for the fifth time, still not convinced it's hanging properly. The department's formal events are rare enough that I'm out of practice with the whole professional dress-up thing.

"Would you stop fidgeting?" Dani slaps my hand away from my collar. "You look fine. Better than fine."

"Easy for you to say. You're not the one getting called up in front of the entire hospital administration." My stomach twists with nerves that have nothing to do with public speaking.

Captain Rivera passes by, clapping me on the shoulder. "Ready for your moment in the spotlight, Bennet?"

"As ready as I'll ever be, sir."

The hospital auditorium buzzes with conversation. Department heads, administrators, and various staff fill the rows of seats. My eyes scan the crowd, finally landing on Liam sitting near the front. He catches my gaze and smiles, giving me a subtle thumbs up that somehow calms the storm in my chest.

Dr. Lawrence Hadley steps to the podium, tapping the microphone. "Good afternoon, everyone. Thank you for joining us for this special recognition ceremony."

I only half-listen as he goes through the formalities, talking about Metropolitan General's commitment to excellence and the importance of recognizing exceptional service. My focus keeps drifting to Liam, whose face shows nothing but pride. Yet something in his eyes seems distant, like part of him is somewhere else entirely.

"And now," Dr. Hadley continues, "I'd like to invite Chief of Emergency Medicine, Dr. Eleanor Vaughn, to present our next commendation."

"It's my pleasure to be here today," she begins, her voice warm but commanding. "While I'm visiting from Boston General, I've had the opportunity to review some extraordinary cases from Metropolitan's emergency services. One paramedic supervisor has consistently demonstrated exceptional clinical judgment, leadership, and patient advocacy."

She continues describing the case that earned me this recognition—a multi-car pileup where I'd coordinated care for eleven patients on scene, including performing a difficult field intubation on a pregnant woman while trapped in an overturned vehicle.

"Noah Bennet's actions that day saved not just one life, but two. His quick thinking and exceptional skill exemplify the highest standards of emergency medical services."

I glance at Liam again. He's beaming, but there's a flash of something in his expression when Dr. Vaughn speaks—guilt? Conflict? It disappears so quickly I can't be sure.

"Noah Bennet, please join me on stage."

My legs carry me forward automatically. I shake Dr. Vaughn's hand as she presents me with a plaque and certificate. The auditorium erupts in applause, loudest from the paramedic section where Dani whistles with two fingers.

"Congratulations," Dr. Vaughn says quietly, her grip firm. "I've heard a lot about you."

"Thank you," I manage, wondering exactly what she's heard and from whom.

I step to the microphone, suddenly aware of how many eyes are on me. "I'm honored, but this recognition belongs to my entire team. We're only as good as the people we work with, and I've been fortunate to work with the best."

My eyes find Liam's again. "And to the incredible emergency department staff who trust us to bring you patients and continue the care we start in the field—thank you for being our partners. This work is about the seamless continuum of care from scene to hospital, and I'm grateful to be part of that chain."

The words feel inadequate, but the applause suggests they're enough. As I return to my seat, I catch Liam's expression—pride mixed with something that looks painfully like goodbye.

After the ceremony, people mill around the reception area with punch and cookies. I'm caught in a revolving door of congratulations until I finally break free and make my way to Liam, who stands conversing with Dr. Vaughn.

"There he is," Liam says as I approach, his smile brightening. "The man of the hour."

"Hardly." I shake my head, embarrassed by the attention. "Just doing my job."

"Mr. Bennet," Dr. Vaughn extends her hand again. "Excellent work. Dr. Winters was just telling me about your exceptional partnership in trauma cases."

"Thank you. And please, it's Noah." I shake her hand, noticing how she studies me with analytical interest.

"Noah," she corrects herself. "Well, I'll leave you to celebrate. Dr. Winters, would you mind joining me for a moment? I need to introduce you to a few important figures within the organization, and discuss a few things." She gives a meaningful nod before gliding away to join a group of administrators.

Liam looks at me helplessly and mouths sorry before following her, leaving me alone.

I watch Liam disappear into the crowd with Dr. Vaughn, leaving me alone with my punch cup and conflicted feelings. The pride from the ceremony mingles with an unsettling suspicion that something's off with Liam. He's been distant lately, distracted in a way I can't quite put my finger on.

"Impressive speech, paramedic."

I turn to find Jason Gauthier standing beside me, looking immaculate in a tailored suit that probably costs more than my monthly rent. His smile doesn't reach his eyes.

"Dr. Gauthier. Didn't expect to see you here." I keep my tone neutral despite the immediate tension tightening my shoulders.

"I wouldn't miss seeing the hospital's power couple in action." He sips his drink, surveying the room with casual disdain. "Though I'm surprised you're not following Liam and Dr. Vaughn. Given their discussions lately, I'd think you'd want to be part of the conversation."

Something in his tone makes me pause. "What discussions?"

Jason's eyebrows rise with practiced surprise. "The fellowship, of course. The one in Boston." He tilts his head, studying my face. "Two years at Boston General under William Chen. It's quite prestigious—career-defining, really. Liam would be foolish to turn it down."

My stomach drops, but I maintain my expression. "Right. That fellowship."

"He hasn't told you." Jason's voice carries false sympathy that makes my skin crawl. "How interesting. I assumed since you two are so..." he waves his hand vaguely, "...connected, that he would have discussed such a significant opportunity with you."

I struggle to keep my face neutral. "We've been busy."

"Mmm. I'm sure." Jason swirls his drink. "The offer came over a week ago. Double his current salary, research funding, teaching position at Harvard Medical. Everything Liam's worked for." He leans closer, lowering his voice. "Dr. Vaughn personally recruited him. She's quite invested in bringing him to Boston."

Each word feels like a physical blow. Liam received a life-changing offer over a week ago and hasn't said a word—all while we've been planning to move in together.

"I'm surprised he's kept you in the dark," Jason continues, his tone dripping with false concern. "Though perhaps not. Liam has always been career-focused. It's what makes him exceptional."

I clench my jaw, refusing to give him the satisfaction of seeing me rattled. "I appreciate the information, Dr. Gauthier, but Liam and I communicate just fine."

"Of course you do." His smile is razor-sharp. "I just thought you should know what you're up against. Boston is quite far from here, and long-distance relationships rarely survive, especially new ones." He checks his watch. "Well, I should mingle. Congratulations again on your... award."

Jason walks away, leaving me standing alone with a punch cup I'm gripping so tightly it's starting to collapse. My mind races, trying to make sense of this revelation. A prestigious fellowship. Boston. Double salary. Harvard. All things Liam would want—should want.

And he hasn't said a word.

I scan the room and spot Liam across the auditorium, deep in conversation with Dr. Vaughn and several other important-looking people in suits. He's smiling, engaged, looking every bit the rising star of emergency medicine that he is.

Suddenly, the pieces start clicking into place—his distraction lately, the way he's avoided certain conversations about our future apartment, how he changed the subject when I brought up signing a lease together last night. The folder I glimpsed him hiding in his desk drawer when I arrived unexpectedly early one evening.

My chest tightens as I realize what this means. Liam has been deliberately keeping this from me. While I've been planning our life together, he's been considering a future that takes him hundreds of miles away.

I set my crumpled cup down on a nearby table and head for the exit. I need air. I need space to think. The recognition plaque in my hand—the one I was so proud of minutes ago—now feels like a hollow consolation prize.

Outside, the cool air hits my face, and I take a deep breath. I lean against the brick wall of the hospital, loosening my tie that suddenly feels like it's choking me.

What hurts most isn't the potential move or even the opportunity itself— it's that Liam didn't trust me enough to share it with me. Instead, I had to hear it from his manipulative ex, of all people.

My phone buzzes in my pocket. A text from Liam: "Where'd you go? Everything ok?"

I stare at the screen, unsure how to respond. Do I confront him here, at his workplace, during what should be a celebration? Do I pretend I don't know and wait for him to tell me—if he ever plans to?

Before I can decide, the hospital doors open, and Liam steps out, concern etched across his face as he spots me against the wall.

I try to compose my face as Liam approaches, but I know he can read me too well. That's the irony—we're so connected he can probably feel my distress from across the room, yet he's kept something this massive from me for over a week.

"Hey, there you are." His smile falters as he gets closer. "I've been looking for you. Everything okay?"

"Having fun in there?" I ask, my voice steadier than I expected.

"It's fine. Just hospital politics." He leans against the wall beside me, our shoulders almost touching. "Sorry about that. Dr. Vaughn wanted to introduce me to some people."

"Yeah, I bet she did." I take a deep breath. "When were you going to tell me about the Boston General fellowship?"

Liam freezes. His face drains of color, and for a moment he looks like one of his patients in shock. "Noah, I—"

"A week, Liam? You've known for over a week?" My voice cracks despite my efforts to keep it level. "We've been planning our future—looking at apartments, talking about moving in together—and all this time you've been considering a job in another country?"

"I was going to tell you." His voice is barely above a whisper. "I've tried several times. I just... I couldn't find the right way."

"The right way?" I push off from the wall, turning to face him fully. "How about 'Hey Noah, I got this amazing opportunity, let's talk about it'? That seems pretty straightforward."

"It's not that simple." He runs a hand through his hair, a gesture I usually find endearing but now reads as evasive. "I've been struggling with this decision. I didn't want to upset you until I knew what I wanted to do."

"So you just left me in the dark instead? Let me make plans for us while you were considering leaving?" The hurt in my voice is unmistakable now. "Do you know how I found out? Jason. Your ex told me, Liam. Do you have any idea how that felt?"

Liam's face crumples. "God, Noah, I'm so sorry. Jason had no right—"

"No, you had no right," I cut him off. "You had no right to keep this from me. We're supposed to be partners. We're supposed to trust each other."

"I do trust you," he insists, reaching for my hand. I pull away.

"No, you don't. If you did, you would have told me about this the moment it happened. We would have figured it out together." I take a step back, creating physical distance to match the emotional chasm opening between us. "What do you want, Liam? What do you actually want in life?"

He stares at me, his mouth opening and closing without sound.

"Is it happiness or your career?" I press. "Because the way I see it, we've been building something real here. Something that makes both of us happy. But if you can throw that away without even discussing it with me..."

Liam's silence stretches between us, heavy and damning. His eyes are filled with conflict, but he doesn't speak. He can't answer the question.

And that's answer enough for me.

"I thought so." My voice comes out hollow. "You know, the hardest part isn't even that you might choose Boston. It's that you didn't respect me enough to include me in the process."

"Noah, please," he finally speaks, his voice breaking. "It's not like that. I care about you more than anything. I just got scared. This fellowship is everything I've worked for professionally, but you... you're everything to me personally. I didn't know how to reconcile those things."

"You start by talking to me," I say, the anger in my voice giving way to sadness. "That's what people who love each other do. They talk through the hard stuff together."

I loosen my tie completely, suddenly feeling suffocated by everything— the formal clothes, the hospital walls looming behind us, the weight of Liam's unspoken decision.

"I need some space," I say, taking another step back. "I can't do this right now."

"Noah, don't go. Please. Let's talk about this."

"Now you want to talk?" I shake my head, a bitter laugh escaping. "I think you've said everything I needed to hear by saying nothing at all."

I turn and walk toward the parking lot, each step feeling heavier than the last. Part of me wants him to run after me, to stop me, to prove that I matter more than his career ambitions. But his footsteps don't follow.

The certificate and plaque I received earlier are still clutched in my hand, the recognition that had made me so proud now tainted by betrayal. As I reach my car, I glance back at the hospital entrance. Liam stands where I left him, watching me go, making no move to follow.

The sadness that washes over me is profound. Not just for what we might be losing, but for what could have been if he'd only trusted in us enough to be honest.

I get into my car and drive away from the hospital, away from Liam, away from the future I thought we were building together.

Chapter 16

Liam

The folder lies open on my desk, its contents mocking me. Dr. Vaughn's business card sits on top of the formal offer letter, the embossed Boston General Hospital logo catching the morning light. Today is the deadline.

I check my phone again—no messages from Noah. I've sent twenty-three texts and called seventeen times over the past week. My last voicemail was pathetic, voice cracking as I begged him to just talk to me.

"Shit," I mutter, running my hand through my hair.

The apartment feels wrong without Noah in it. I've grown accustomed to his presence—his shoes by the door, his favorite mug in the sink, his scent on my pillows. Now there's just emptiness and the weight of my indecision.

I dial Noah's number again, holding my breath through each ring until his voicemail picks up.

"Noah, it's me. Again. Today's the deadline for the Boston offer and I—I don't know what to do. Please call me back. Please."

My finger hovers over the end call button, but I can't press it yet.

"I miss you," I add, voice barely above a whisper before hanging up.

The clock on my microwave reads 9:17 AM. I have until 5:00 PM to email Dr. Vaughn my decision. Eight hours to determine the trajectory of my career and my heart.

I grab my keys and head for the door. If Noah won't answer my calls, I'll try his apartment again. I've been there three times this week already, knocking until my knuckles hurt, but today feels different. Today everything changes, one way or another.

Noah's building is a fifteen-minute drive from mine. Each minute feels like an hour as my mind races through every possible scenario. What if he's not there? What if he refuses to see me? What if this is truly over?

I park haphazardly and sprint to his door, my heart pounding against my ribcage. Three sharp knocks. Silence. Three more.

"Noah, please. I know you're in there. Your car's outside."

Nothing.

"I'm not leaving until you talk to me."

I slide down against the door, sitting on his welcome mat—the one we picked out together at a home goods store two weeks ago. It feels like a lifetime has passed since then.

"Fine. If you won't talk, just listen," I say, leaning my head back against the door. "I should have told you about Boston the minute Dr. Vaughn offered it. I was wrong to keep it from you. I was scared—terrified, actually—of having to choose."

My voice echoes slightly in the empty hallway.

"The fellowship is everything I've worked for professionally. But you—you're everything I never knew I needed personally."

I pull the offer letter from my jacket pocket, unfolding it carefully.

"Two years at Boston General. Double my current salary. Research funding. Teaching position at Harvard Medical. It's the opportunity of a lifetime."

I trace the signature line with my finger, the blank space where my name should go.

"But none of it matters without you. I've spent my entire career building walls, keeping everyone at a distance because it felt safer. Then you showed up and somehow knew exactly how to find your way through."

The door remains silent, unyielding.

"Noah, I love you. I've never said that to anyone before, not like this. And I'm terrified that I've ruined the best thing that's ever happened to me because I was too afraid to be honest with you."

My phone vibrates in my pocket—a text notification. My heart leaps until I see it's from Dr. Vaughn: "Looking forward to your decision by EOD. Let me know if you have any final questions."

I pocket the phone and stand up, my resolve hardening.

"I'm going to Metropolitan now. I need to check on my father, then I have a shift. But I'll be back tonight, Noah. And tomorrow. And the next day. For as long as it takes."

I press my palm flat against the door, imagining Noah on the other side.

"I won't give up on us."

The hospital buzzes with its usual controlled chaos when I arrive. Mira spots me from the nurses' station and her expression shifts from greeting to concern.

"You look like hell," she says, handing me a patient chart.

"Thanks. Feel like it too."

"Noah?" she asks, though she already knows the answer.

I nod, flipping through the chart without really seeing it.

"He's hurting, Liam. You kept something huge from him while planning a future together."

"I know," I say, rubbing my eyes. "Today's the deadline for the fellowship."

"And?"

"And I have no idea what to do."

Mira's eyes soften. "Yes, you do. You're just afraid to admit it."

Before I can respond, my pager beeps. Robert Winters, room 412. My father needs me.

I find him sitting up in bed, looking frailer than last week. The aggressive chemotherapy protocol Dr. Kang started has taken its toll.

"You came," he says, surprise evident in his voice.

"I'm your doctor," I reply automatically, checking his vitals on the monitor.

"No, Melissa is my doctor. You're my son who happens to be a doctor."

I ignore the comment, reviewing his chart. "Your white count is low. They'll need to adjust the chemo dosage."

"Liam." His voice is gentle but firm. "Sit down for a minute."

Something in his tone makes me comply. I perch on the edge of the visitor's chair.

"What's wrong?" he asks.

I almost laugh. "You're asking me what's wrong? You're the one with pancreatic cancer."

"And you're the one who looks like you've lost your best friend." He studies my face. "Or something more than a friend?"

The question catches me off guard. We don't talk about personal things. We barely talk at all.

"It's nothing," I say, standing up.

"Noah hasn't been by in days," Robert observes. "He used to come with you every time."

I freeze, surprised he noticed. "How did you—"

"I may be dying, but I'm not blind." A small smile crosses his face. "He loves you. Anyone can see that."

"Loved," I correct him, the past tense painful on my tongue. "I messed up."

Robert nods slowly. "I'm familiar with that feeling."

Our eyes meet, and for a moment, I see myself in him—the stubbornness, the pride, the fear of vulnerability.

"I have to make a decision today," I say, surprising myself by continuing. "A fellowship in Boston. It's everything I've worked for, but—"

"But Noah isn't in Boston," he finishes for me.

"I didn't tell him about it. Not until he found out from someone else."

Robert sighs. "You know, your mother used to say I was too afraid to be happy. That I'd sabotage any chance at joy because I didn't believe I deserved it." He looks out the window. "She was right."

The admission hangs between us.

"Don't make my mistakes, Liam. Don't push away the people who matter most because you're afraid."

My pager beeps again—trauma alert in the ER. I stand up, oddly grateful for the interruption.

"I have to go."

Robert nods. "Just remember—careers end. Fellowships finish. But regret? That lasts forever."

I leave his room with his words echoing in my head, suddenly clear about what I need to do.

* * *

I rush through the trauma case—a motorcycle accident that thankfully looks worse than it is. The rider's protective gear saved him from anything beyond a dislocated shoulder and some road rash. As I finish the discharge paperwork, my mind keeps circling back to my father's words.

"Regret lasts forever."

I check my watch. Two hours until my deadline with Dr. Vaughn. My heart pounds as I pull out my phone and send her a message: "Need to speak with you before I give my decision. Available now?"

Her response comes quickly: "In conference room C for the next hour."

I hand off my patients to Dr. Chen, ignoring his questioning look, and make my way upstairs. Each step feels heavier than the last, but my resolve strengthens. For once in my life, I'm going to choose what I truly want, not what I think I should want.

Dr. Eleanor Vaughn sits at the conference table, laptop open, glasses perched on her nose. She smiles when I enter, gesturing to the chair across from her.

"Liam, I was hoping to hear from you today." Her Boston accent makes my name sound like "Lee-um." "Have you made your decision about the fellowship?"

I take a deep breath. "I have some questions first."

"Of course." She closes her laptop, giving me her full attention.

"The position is in Boston, but I have... connections here that are important to me."

She nods. "Personal ties can be difficult, but this is a career-defining opportunity."

"What if those ties could come with me?" I ask, my mouth suddenly dry. "I'm seeing someone—Noah Bennet. He's a paramedic supervisor here."

Dr. Vaughn's expression shifts subtly. "I see, the man we gave the award to."

"He's exceptional at what he does. Boston General would be lucky to have him." The words rush out. "If there was a position for him, with better compensation than he currently receives, I would accept the fellowship immediately."

She leans back, studying me. "Liam, while I appreciate your dedication to your relationship, that's not how these appointments work. We've selected you based on your qualifications, not as part of a package deal."

"I understand that, but—"

"Boston General has its own established EMS system with supervisors already in place. Creating a position specifically to accommodate your partner's career would be... unprecedented."

"So that's a no?" I ask, though I already know the answer.

Dr. Vaughn sighs. "It's not feasible, I'm afraid." She leans forward. "But Liam, this fellowship is the next big step in your career. The connections you'll make, the research opportunities, the prestige of Harvard Medical—these are things most emergency physicians only dream about."

"I know."

"And the salary," she continues, "would set you up for financial security that most doctors your age simply don't have."

I nod, acknowledging the truth in her words.

"Long-distance relationships can work," she offers. "Boston to here is just a short flight. Many couples manage it."

I think about Noah—his laugh, his intuitive understanding of me, the way we move together like we've known each other for lifetimes instead of months. I think about waking up without him, coming home to an empty apartment, trying to share my day over FaceTime instead of across a dinner table.

"I can't accept the position," I say, the words bringing unexpected relief.

Dr. Vaughn's eyebrows shoot up. "Liam, I don't think you understand what you're turning down. This fellowship could define your entire career trajectory."

"I understand exactly what I'm turning down," I reply, my voice steadier than I expected. "And I'm choosing something else."

"This is about a relationship that's, what, a few months old?" Her tone carries a hint of dismissal. "That's not a rational basis for a decision of this magnitude."

"With all due respect, Dr. Vaughn, it's not just about the relationship's duration. It's about its quality." I stand up, suddenly eager to be done with this conversation. "It's not worth throwing away my happiness just for money or prestige."

"You're making a mistake," she says, her disappointment evident. "An opportunity like this won't come around again."

"Maybe not," I concede. "But neither will Noah."

She shakes her head. "I urge you to reconsider. Take the weekend to think it over. Talk to your mentors. I can extend the deadline until Monday."

"That's generous, but my answer won't change." I move toward the door, then turn back. "Thank you for considering me for the position. It means a lot that you thought I was qualified."

Dr. Vaughn looks genuinely perplexed. "I've never had a candidate turn down this fellowship before."

"Then I guess I'm making history," I say with a small smile.

As I walk out of the conference room, my phone buzzes with a text from Mira: "Did you do it? What did you decide?"

I type back: "Staying here. Some things are worth more than a fellowship."

I head toward the elevator, already planning what I'll say when I show up at Noah's door tonight. For the first time in days, I feel like I can breathe again.

Chapter 17

Noah

The lease sits on my kitchen table like a bomb that never went off. Our names—Noah Bennet and Liam Winters—side by side in black ink on crisp white paper. The apartment on Maple Street. The one with the bay windows Liam loved and the kitchen island I couldn't wait to cook on. Two signatures binding us to a future that feels like it's crumbling before it even began.

I trace my finger over Liam's name. Three days since I walked away from him outside the hospital. Three days of silence that feel like three years.

"You should eat something," Marcus says, placing a plate of scrambled eggs beside me.

I push it away. "Not hungry."

"Noah, come on. You've barely touched food since—"

"Since I found out my boyfriend was planning to leave me for Boston?" The words taste bitter. "Since I discovered everyone at the hospital knew about this fellowship except me?"

Marcus sits across from me, his expression careful. "Did you actually let him explain?"

"What's there to explain? He had a week—over a week—to tell me. We were making plans to build a life together while he was interviewing for jobs in another state."

I stand up and walk to the window, staring out at nothing. The world outside keeps moving. People rushing to work, laughing, living their lives. Meanwhile, I feel stuck in this moment of betrayal, replaying Jason's smug face as he dropped the Boston bomb on me.

My phone lights up with a text from Dani: *Shift starts in 30. You coming in today?*

I haven't called out sick since I started at Metro. But yesterday, I couldn't face the possibility of seeing Liam in those hallways. Today doesn't feel any different.

Be there soon, I type back anyway. Work is the only thing that might distract me from this hollow feeling in my chest.

I shower and dress mechanically. My paramedic uniform feels heavier than usual. As I grab my keys, my eyes catch on Liam's toothbrush in my bathroom. The one he keeps here—kept here—for all those nights we couldn't bear to be apart. I should throw it away. Instead, I close the door and leave it there.

The drive to the station is a blur. Songs on the radio that Liam and I used to sing along to now feel like tiny daggers. I switch it off, preferring silence.

"You look like shit," Dani says when I arrive, handing me a coffee.

"Thanks for the vote of confidence."

She studies my face. "Have you talked to him?"

"Nothing to talk about."

"Noah—"

"Let's just focus on work, okay?"

The day passes in a fog. We respond to calls—a senior with chest pain, a kid with a broken arm, a fender bender on Main Street. I go through the motions, checking vitals, administering care, transporting patients. But something's missing. The spark that used to drive me, the passion I've always had for this job—it's dimmed somehow.

"You're not yourself today," an elderly woman tells me as I check her blood pressure after a fall. "Your smile doesn't reach your eyes."

I force a better one. "Just tired, ma'am."

But she pats my hand knowingly. "That's heartbreak, young man. I've seen it enough to recognize it."

I don't confirm or deny, just finish my assessment and help her into the ambulance.

By mid-afternoon, we get a call to Metropolitan General. My stomach knots as we pull up to the ER bay. Part of me hopes to see him. Part of me dreads it. But Liam isn't there—Dr. Kapoor meets us instead, and I feel both relief and disappointment crash over me in equal measure.

"How are you holding up?" She asks quietly as we transfer the patient.

"I'm fine." The lie comes easily now after repeating it all day.

"He's not doing well either, if that helps."

It doesn't. The thought of Liam suffering only makes me feel worse, not better. Because despite everything, I still love him. And that's what makes this so damn hard.

After shift, I find myself driving past the Maple Street apartment building. Our building—or what should have been our building. I park across the street and just stare up at the third-floor windows. We had planned where the couch would go. Which bedroom would be ours. How we'd set up a small home office in the spare room for Liam's research.

All those plans, all those dreams, built on what feels like quicksand.

Back at my apartment, I pull out the bottle of wine we bought to celebrate signing the lease. The one we never opened because we got called into that trauma. I pour a glass and sit back at the table with the lease.

"What am I supposed to do now?" I ask the empty room.

The silence offers no answers. My apartment feels wrong without Liam in it. Too quiet. Too empty. I've grown so accustomed to his presence—the way he hums when he reads, how he always leaves his socks on the floor, the sound of his breathing when he sleeps beside me.

I pull out my phone and stare at our text thread. My thumb hovers over the keyboard, but what would I even say? That I'm angry? That I'm hurt? That despite everything, I miss him like I'd miss oxygen?

Instead, I set the phone down and take another sip of wine. The lease stares back at me, mocking what almost was.

The truth is, my life made more sense with Liam in it. Everything clicked into place when we were together, like we'd been designed as two parts of the same whole. That connection we felt from the first moment—it wasn't just professional. It was something deeper, something I've never experienced with anyone else.

And now there's just this emptiness where he used to be.

Chapter 18

Liam

I've been standing outside Noah's apartment building for twenty minutes, pacing back and forth like a madman. My white coat is still on from my shift—I came straight here, not even stopping to change. The bouquet of wildflowers I hastily purchased from the hospital gift shop is already starting to wilt in my nervous grip.

This is ridiculous. I'm a thirty-four-year-old doctor who regularly makes life-or-death decisions, yet here I am, terrified to press the buzzer to Noah's apartment.

I take a deep breath and pull out my phone instead. My thumbs hover over the screen.

I'm outside. Please talk to me.

No response. I wait five more minutes, then try again.

Noah, I know I messed up. I just need five minutes.

Still nothing.

Desperate times call for desperate measures.

I scan the ground around me, finding a few small pebbles near a landscaped area. I pick them up, walk back, and aim for Noah's second-floor window. The first pebble misses completely. The second makes a pathetic little tap that wouldn't wake a mouse.

"What the hell am I doing?" I mutter to myself.

An elderly woman walking her dog gives me a concerned look as she passes by.

Fine. If this is what it takes.

I pull out my phone again and scroll to my music app. I find the song—the one that was playing at the diner when we had our first date, before Emily's allergic reaction interrupted us. It's some cheesy 80s power ballad that Noah loves.

I crank the volume to maximum and hold my phone above my head, John Cusack style.

The music blares across the quiet residential street. Windows from neighboring apartments begin to open. Someone shouts at me to shut up. I ignore them, my eyes fixed on Noah's window.

"Noah!" I shout between verses. "Noah Bennet! I love you!"

More windows open. More complaints. I don't care.

"I'm not leaving until you talk to me!"

Finally, Noah's window slides open. He leans out, hair disheveled, eyes red-rimmed. My heart breaks and soars simultaneously at the sight of him.

"Are you insane?" he calls down, but there's a hint of something other than anger in his voice.

"Completely," I answer. "About you."

"You're disturbing my neighbors."

"I'll disturb the entire city if that's what it takes."

Noah shakes his head, but I can see the corner of his mouth twitch. "Five minutes," he says finally. "I'll buzz you up."

The intercom buzzes and I practically run to the door. The elevator ride to the second floor feels eternal. When Noah opens his door, he's standing with arms crossed, keeping a careful distance.

"You look terrible," he says.

"I feel terrible." I hold out the sad bouquet. "These are for you."

He takes them reluctantly. "Thanks."

"Can I come in? Please?"

Noah steps aside, allowing me into the apartment I've spent so many nights in. It feels both familiar and foreign now.

"Five minutes," he reminds me.

I nod, suddenly unsure where to begin. All my rehearsed speeches evaporate.

"I turned down the fellowship," I blurt out.

Noah's eyes widen. "What?"

"I told Dr. Vaughn no. Yesterday."

"But—why would you do that? It's the opportunity of a lifetime."

I step closer, desperate to touch him but restraining myself. "Because it's not worth losing you. Nothing is."

"Liam—"

"No, please, let me finish." I take a deep breath. "I asked her if there was any way you could come with me, if she could find a position for you too. She said no."

"You asked that?"

"Of course I did. But the moment she said it wasn't possible, I knew my answer. I don't want Boston, Noah. I want you."

Noah's arms uncross, his posture softening slightly. "Why didn't you tell me about it from the beginning?"

I sink onto his couch, my legs suddenly weak. "Because I was terrified. When Dr. Vaughn first made the offer, I was flattered, excited even. But then I went home to you that night, and you were talking about apartments and our future, and I just... froze."

"You didn't trust me enough to have an adult conversation about it?"

"It wasn't about trust. It was about fear." I look up at him, willing him to understand. "Every relationship I've ever had has ended because of my career. When Jason left, it was because I wasn't ambitious enough, wasn't willing to play hospital politics to advance. And here was this fellowship—the exact thing he would have wanted me to take—and all I could think was that it would cost me you."

Noah sits beside me, not touching, but closer. "So you just decided not to tell me?"

"I convinced myself I needed time to figure out how to handle it. But really, I was just scared. Paralyzed by the thought of losing you."

"You almost lost me anyway by keeping it secret."

"I know. I was an idiot." I gather my courage and reach for his hand. He doesn't pull away. "Noah, I want everything with you. The apartment on Maple Street. A house with a white picket fence someday. A dog. Kids—1.5 of them, statistically speaking." This earns me a small smile. "I want to grow old arguing about whose turn it is to take out the trash and who gets the last piece of pizza."

"That's a lot of wants," Noah says softly.

"I've never wanted anything more in my life. I've spent years building walls around myself, focusing on my career because it felt safer than risking my heart. Then you walked into my ER, and somehow you just... knew me. Better than I know myself sometimes."

Noah's fingers tighten around mine. "I was so hurt when Jason told me."

"I know. And I'm so sorry. I should have been the one to tell you. I should have trusted what we have."

"And what do we have, Liam?"

I look into his eyes, all pretense gone. "Everything. At least, that's what it feels like to me."

I hold Noah's gaze, my heart hammering against my ribs. The silence between us stretches, thick with possibility and fear. I've laid myself bare—my hopes, my mistakes, my future—all of it resting in his hands.

"I want to forgive you," Noah finally says, his voice rough with emotion. "But Liam, you have to understand what this did to me."

"I do," I whisper, squeezing his hand.

"No, I need you to really hear this." He shifts to face me directly. "When Jason told me about Boston, it wasn't just that you kept a secret. It felt like you were making plans to leave me behind. Like what we have wasn't important enough to even discuss."

The pain in his eyes cuts deeper than any surgical blade I've ever wielded.

"I'm listening," I say, fighting to keep my voice steady.

"I can forgive this once, Liam. I can understand being scared." His eyes harden slightly. "But if you ever shut me out like this again, we're done. No second chances. No grand gestures with wilting flowers and 80s music. I need a partner who trusts me enough to share the hard stuff, not just the easy parts."

The ultimatum hangs between us. It's fair—more than fair—and I know I don't deserve his forgiveness at all.

"I understand," I manage to say, my vision blurring with tears. "I promise, Noah. Never again."

Something in my face must convince him because his expression softens. "Okay."

That single word—okay—breaks the dam inside me. Tears stream down my face as relief crashes through my body. I launch myself into his arms, not caring how desperate I look.

"I'm so sorry," I murmur against his neck. "I love you so much."

His arms wrap around me, strong and familiar, and I feel his body shake slightly with his own emotion.

"I missed you," he confesses, his voice cracking. When I pull back to look at him, tears are tracking down his cheeks too. "Don't you ever disappear on me like that again."

"Never," I promise, cupping his face in my hands. I kiss him, tasting the salt of our mingled tears. It's messy and imperfect and absolutely perfect.

Noah's hands tighten on my waist, pulling me closer. The kiss deepens, transforms from reunion to something hungrier. I've missed this—missed him—so much that every nerve ending in my body seems to ignite at his touch.

He breaks the kiss, breathing hard. "I'm still mad at you," he says, but his hands are already sliding under my shirt.

"I know," I whisper, pressing my forehead against his. "You have every right to be."

"But I missed you more than I'm angry." His fingers trace patterns on my skin. "I couldn't sleep without you here."

"Me neither." I kiss him again, pouring every ounce of apology and love into it. "Let me show you how sorry I am."

Noah stands, pulling me up with him. Without a word, he leads me down the familiar hallway to his bedroom. The room is a mess—clothes scattered across the floor, bed unmade, takeout containers on the nightstand. It's so unlike Noah's usual tidiness that I realize just how much our separation affected him.

He turns to me, vulnerability written across his face. "I'm not sure I'm ready to talk about everything yet."

"We don't have to talk," I say, reaching for him.

Our clothes practically disintegrate off our bodies, the desire between us too potent to be contained. Our naked forms collide, and I feel Noah's hard length press against my entrance. His hands grip my hips, guiding me onto all fours as he positions himself and slicks up his cock with the lube on his bedside table.

With a primal growl, he slides inside me in one deep, forceful thrust. I gasp at the intensity of the sensation, but it only spurs him on. His hips pound relentlessly into mine, each thrust driving him deeper and deeper until I can't tell where he ends and I begin as he reclaims me. His hands roam over my body, leaving a trail of goosebumps in their wake. He grabs my hips roughly, angling his thrusts to hit that spot inside me that makes stars explode behind my eyelids. "God, Liam," he growls in my ear, "I want to hear you beg for it."

His words fan the flames of desire within me. "Please," I pant, my voice hoarse with need. "Please, Noah... don't stop."

He obliges, but only by increasing the pace and depth of his thrusts. Each powerful stroke sends shockwaves of pleasure through my entire body. I can feel myself teetering on the edge of orgasm, but Noah shows no signs of stopping. "Beg me for more," he demands, his voice a deep rumble in my ear. "Oh god," I moan, my breath coming in ragged gasps. "More... please... don't stop."

Noah chuckles darkly and obliges me by slamming even deeper inside me. His fingers dig into my hips as he grinds against my prostate relentlessly. The sensation is almost too much to bear—but I don't want it to end. Ever. "Say it again," he pants out between thrusts. "Tell me how much you need this." "I-I need you so fucking much!" I cry out as pleasure courses through every nerve ending in my body. "Never stop... never leave me again." With those words echoing between us, we both tip over the edge together—our cries mingling as we spill our release onto the sheets beneath us.

As our bodies finally still, our breaths coming in ragged gasps, Noah's words cut through the haze of pleasure. "I was going to sign the lease for the Maple Street apartment," he says quietly, his voice thick with emotion. "The day after... after everything happened."

My heart constricts at the mention of what might have been. I turn over onto my side, facing him as I card my fingers through his damp hair. "I know," I whisper, my voice barely above a whisper. "I remember."

I lift my head to look at him. "Is it still available?"

"I don't know. I haven't called them back."

"We could call tomorrow," I suggest hesitantly. "If you still want to."

Noah's arms tighten around me. "I still want everything with you, Liam. That hasn't changed."

Relief washes through me. "Even the 1.5 statistical children?"

He laughs, the sound vibrating against my cheek. "Even them. Though I think we should round up to two."

"Two it is," I agree, pressing a kiss to his chest, right over his heart.

We fall silent again, content to simply be together. The world outside this room—the hospital, my father's illness, Jason's unwelcome presence—all of it can wait. For now, we've found our way back to each other, and that's enough.

Epilogue

Six Months Later

Noah

The alarm chirps at 5:30 AM, and I silence it before it wakes Liam. Early shift today. I slide out from under his arm, smiling at how he's sprawled across our bed—our bed, in our apartment. Six months living together, and that thought still gives me a little thrill.

I pad quietly through our bedroom, careful not to stub my toe on the antique medical cabinet we found at that flea market last month. The morning light filters through the blinds of our Maple Street apartment, casting stripes across the hardwood floors we spent a weekend refinishing together.

In the kitchen, I start the coffee maker—programmed exactly how Liam likes it—and pull out ingredients for a quick breakfast. His shift starts three hours after mine today, which means I'll miss him at the hospital. These offset schedules happen about twice a week, but we've learned to make it work.

My phone buzzes with a text from Dani: *Running 5 late. Traffic on Elm.*

I text back: *No worries. Making breakfast.*

While the eggs cook, I notice the framed photo on our refrigerator—Liam and me at the hospital fundraiser gala last month, both in tuxedos, his arm around my waist. Next to it is the schedule we created together, color-coded for our shifts, family dinners (Robert joins us every other Sunday now), and date nights that we protect fiercely.

I hear the shuffle of feet behind me and turn to find Liam, hair mussed from sleep, wearing only boxers and one of my old t-shirts.

"You're up early," I say, flipping the eggs. "Go back to sleep. You've got three more hours."

He wraps his arms around my waist from behind, pressing his face between my shoulder blades. "Smelled coffee. Missed you."

I turn in his embrace, kissing him softly. "I made enough for two."

"My hero." He yawns, reaching for a mug. "What's your day look like?"

"Standard shift, then meeting with Rivera about the new protocols. Should be home by seven." I plate the eggs and toast. "You?"

"ER until eight, but Dr. Chen's letting me leave early if it's quiet. Oh—" He pauses, sipping his coffee. "Dad wants to know if we can move dinner to Saturday instead of Sunday. His chemo schedule changed."

I nod, making a mental note. "Tell him that's fine."

Robert's cancer treatments have been rough, but he's responding well. The relationship between him and Liam has evolved into something neither of them expected—not perfect, but healing. I've come to appreciate Robert's dry humor and the way he tries, really tries, to be present now.

"I'll pick up groceries for dinner," Liam says, stealing a bite from my plate.

"Get your own, thief." I swat his hand playfully.

"Why would I when yours tastes better?" He grins, that crooked smile that still makes my heart skip.

We eat together in comfortable silence for a few minutes. This is one of my favorite parts of living together—these quiet, ordinary moments that feel extraordinary because we're sharing them.

"You know what today is?" I ask.

Liam looks up, thinking. "Thursday?"

"Six months since we moved in." I reach across the table, taking his hand. "Best decision I ever made."

His expression softens. "Even with my terrible sock-folding technique?"

"Even with that." I squeeze his hand. "Though if you could stop leaving wet towels on the bed, that would be great."

"And if you could remember to replace the toilet paper roll..."

"Touché." I stand, clearing our plates. "I've got to get going. Dani's already running late."

Liam follows me to the door, handing me my jacket. "Be safe out there. I don't want to see you in my ER today."

"No promises. You know how irresistible you are in those scrubs." I kiss him goodbye, lingering a moment longer than necessary.

"I love you," he says against my lips.

"Love you more."

My shift flies by—three cardiac calls, a diabetic emergency, and a minor fender bender. Around noon, I bring an elderly woman with a broken hip to Metro General. As we wheel her through the ER doors, I scan the department automatically, looking for Liam.

He's at the nurses' station, reviewing a chart with Dr. Chen. Our eyes meet, and he gives me a professional nod, though I catch the slight upturn of his lips. We've perfected this dance—maintaining professionalism at work while acknowledging our connection.

"Seventy-eight-year-old female, mechanical fall at home, suspected right hip fracture," I report as we transfer the patient. "Vitals stable, pain at 7/10, controlled with fentanyl en route."

"Thank you, Supervisor Bennet," Liam says formally, though his eyes hold warmth only I can see. "We'll take it from here."

As I'm leaving, he passes me a patient chart, our fingers brushing deliberately. "Discharge papers for your last drop-off," he says, voice professional but low. Inside the folder is a small note: *Leftover lasagna in the fridge for your lunch. Text me when you're on break.* These small gestures mean everything. Six months in, and we've found our rhythm—the balance between our professional responsibilities and personal connection.

After shift, I stop by the store for Robert's favorite ice cream before heading home. Our apartment welcomes me with the smell of garlic and herbs. Liam's cooking tonight.

"Honey, I'm home," I call out, hanging my jacket on the hook beside his.

Liam appears from the kitchen, wooden spoon in hand. "How was your day, dear?" he asks with exaggerated domesticity.

"Saved lives, fought traffic, the usual." I hold up the ice cream. "For Saturday."

"Dad will be thrilled." He returns to the stove as I follow him into the kitchen. "I made that chicken thing you like."

"The one with the sauce?"

"That's the one."

I wrap my arms around him from behind, mirroring how he held me this morning. "This is nice," I murmur into his shoulder. "Coming home to you. Having dinner ready."

"Even if we sometimes go days barely seeing each other?" He stirs the sauce.

"Even then." I kiss his neck. "Especially then. Makes moments like this more precious."

He turns in my arms. "Six months ago, I almost threw this away."

"But you didn't." I touch his face. "And now look at us. Domestic bliss."

"Complete with bickering over whose turn it is to clean the bathroom." He laughs.

"I wouldn't have it any other way."

And it's true. The professional respect, the personal love, the life we're building—it's everything I never knew I needed. Six months in, and every day I'm more certain: this is exactly where I'm meant to be.

***

Liam

I tug my gloves on with practiced efficiency as the trauma bay fills with organized chaos. The paramedics wheel in a woman with multiple stab wounds, her vitals flashing critical numbers on the portable monitor.

"Twenty-eight-year-old female, three stab wounds to the abdomen," Noah announces, his voice steady as he locks eyes with me across the gurney. "BP 90/60 and dropping, pulse 120, resps shallow at 24. Two large-bore IVs running wide, one liter in, O-neg hanging."

I nod, already processing the information as we transfer her to the trauma bed. "Let's get a trauma panel, type and cross for four units, and prep for an ex-lap. Dr. Chen, can you ultrasound the abdomen?"

Noah moves to the head of the bed, already preparing to assist with airway management before I even ask. Six months of living together, and over a year since we first met in this very trauma room, our connection has only deepened. We move in perfect synchrony, anticipating each other's needs without words.

"Fluid in Morrison's pouch," Dr. Chen confirms. "Definite intraperitoneal bleeding."

"She's dropping," Noah says, eyes on the monitor. "BP 80/50."

"Push another bolus and call OR 2," I direct the team. "Let's get her intubated. Noah—"

He's already reaching for the laryngoscope, setting up for rapid sequence intubation. "Meds are ready."

The trauma team moves around us like water flowing around two fixed points. Noah and I function as a single unit, our movements choreographed by something beyond training or familiarity. It's that same inexplicable connection we felt that first day, now refined and strengthened by time.

"I'm in," Noah says after the intubation. "Good bilateral breath sounds."

"Excellent work," I murmur, catching his eye with a brief professional nod that carries deeper meaning only he can read.

As we prepare the patient for transport to the OR, I notice Mira watching us with a knowing smile. She's witnessed our journey from that first bewildering connection to now—partners in every sense.

"Dr. Winters, do you want to accompany to the OR?" Dr. Hayes asks, arriving to take over the surgical case.

"No need. She's stabilizing with the transfusion. I'll stay for the next incoming trauma." I sign off on the chart. "Noah, can you help transport?"

"On it," he replies, moving to the head of the gurney.

As the team wheels our patient toward the elevator, I take a moment to breathe. This trauma room holds so much history for us. I remember standing in this exact spot the first time Noah brought in a patient, feeling that immediate, inexplicable pull toward him. Back then, I'd tried to rationalize it away. Now, I know better.

Noah returns fifteen minutes later, finding me updating charts at the trauma desk.

"Just like old times," he says, leaning against the counter beside me. "Except better."

I smile, feeling that familiar warmth spread through my chest. "Much better."

"Remember the first time we worked together in here?" Noah asks, his voice low enough that only I can hear. "I thought I was losing my mind."

"You and me both." I glance around to ensure we're not being overheard. "I kept telling myself it was just good professional chemistry."

Noah laughs. "Is that what the kids are calling it these days?"

The trauma phone rings, interrupting our moment. I answer it quickly, listening to the incoming report before hanging up.

"Two-car MVA, five minutes out. One critical with head trauma."

Noah straightens, already shifting back into professional mode. "I'll get the rapid infuser ready."

As he moves away, I allow myself a moment to appreciate how far we've come. Six months ago, I nearly lost him by keeping the Boston fellowship secret. Now, I can't imagine any career advancement being worth sacrificing what we have.

I think back to Jason's last day at Metro General, about two weeks after Noah and I reconciled. Jason had cornered me in the doctors' lounge, his expression sour.

"So you're really choosing the paramedic over your career?" he'd asked, voice dripping with condescension.

"I'm choosing happiness," I'd replied simply. "And for the record, Noah is a paramedic supervisor with more compassion and integrity than you'll ever have."

Jason had scoffed, but I saw the moment he realized he'd lost—not just me, but any power he thought he had over me. He left the hospital the next day, cutting his visiting surgeon rotation short. I heard through the grapevine that he'd returned to Ottawa, claiming Metro General wasn't challenging enough.

The ambulance bay doors slide open, pulling me back to the present. Noah's team rushes in with our MVA victim, and we fall back into our seamless rhythm. In the controlled chaos of the trauma room, our connection shines brightest—two people operating as one, saving lives together.

"GCS 7," Noah reports. "Pupils equal but sluggish. Obvious deformity to the left temporal region with raccoon eyes developing."

I'm already calling for a STAT head CT as we work to stabilize the patient. Noah anticipates my every move, handing me equipment before I ask, adjusting ventilator settings as I assess the patient's neurological status.

"Remember when people used to stare at us working together?" Noah whispers as we wait for neurosurgery.

I smile behind my mask. "They still do. They've just gotten better at hiding it."

The truth is, what we have is rare—both professionally and personally. That first inexplicable connection in this trauma room led to the most important relationship of my life. And every day, every patient, every moment working alongside Noah only confirms what I've known since that first day: some connections are meant to be.

Author's Note

Hi there,

Thanks for reading my novel *Emergency Contact*! I hope you had as much fun reading it as I did writing it. If you truly enjoyed the story, please feel free to leave an honest review on the website of your choice. Reviews greatly influence the reading decisions of others, and help independent authors stand out from the crowd.

For release announcements, advanced reader signup opportunities, and more please signup for my newsletter at www.cgmacington.ca.

Happy Reading!
C.G. Macington

Other Works Available

Elemental: Forgotten Heritage

18-year-old orphan Noah lives a simple life in poverty with his grandmother. This changes overnight, as he comes into an elemental inheritance with god-imbued powers and learns he is the last descendant of an ancient line of royal magic. Noah is swept into a journey fleeing from a corrupted ruler hellbent on destroying the last remnants of Noah's lineage. His journey is filled with magic, danger, and a forbidden love with a man from his dreams. Now Noah's choices will save - or destroy - the Kingdom and those he loves.

Defying the Crown

When damaged hearts collide, can love overcome secrets?
Daniel isn't looking for love. After a devastating betrayal left him wary of relationships, he's focused on healing and rebuilding his life in New York City. But fate has other plans when a charming Danish stranger named Harald slides into his DMs.
Harald carries the weight of a crown he's not sure he can bear. As Denmark's heir apparent, he's trapped between duty and desire, forced to hide his true self behind palace walls. When he connects with Daniel online, he sees a chance at real happiness—if only he can keep his royal identity secret.
As their whirlwind romance spans from Manhattan's bustling streets to Copenhagen's historic charm, their connection deepens into something neither expected. But with Harald's throne-sized secret threatening to tear them apart, and Daniel's trust hanging by a thread, can their love survive the truth?
A steamy, contemporary gay romance about finding the courage to love yourself, trust again, and fight for what matters—crown or no crown.